FULL STEAM

Cassie Miles

A KISMET™ Romance

 METEOR PUBLISHING CORPORATION
Bensalem, Pennsylvania

KISMET™ is a trademark of Meteor Publishing Corporation

Copyright © 1990 Kay Bergstrom
Cover Art copyright © 1990 Les Katz

First Printing September 1990.

ISBN: 1-878702-09-2

Printed in the United States of America

CASSIE MILES

Cassie Miles lives in Denver with her two daughters and too many dogs and is happy to be a westerner. Cassie has published several contemporary romance and intrigue novels. When not writing herself, she teaches novel writing classes and was Colorado Romance Writer of the Year in 1984. "Sunset and moonrise in the Rocky Mountains is pure romance. Denver is where you can touch the clouds."

ONE

The clutter in Darcy Conway's office was similar to an explosion in a time machine.

Manilla folders sprawled across the antique Persian rug. Darcy's lavender parka was flung round the neck of a marble bust. A computer mingled shamelessly with a clutter of carnival glass vases and sepia photographs in gilt frames.

Darcy stood at the bay window, hands on hips, and studied the chaos. Soft winter light diffused through the lead panes, highlighting her silhouette— a tumbled-down topknot of curly black hair, an ivory cameo profile and a long, graceful neck. Though she wore Levis and a baggy sweatshirt, her erect posture and delicate bone structure seemed old-fashioned as a painted doll with bow lips and china blue eyes.

She knelt and picked up a brightly painted, wooden train engine—*The Little Engine that Could.*

If the Little Engine could fight its way to the top of an insurmountable mountain, she could surely manage to get her office packed before the movers arrived tomorrow morning. She gave the toy train a push across the hardwood floor. *I think I can. I think I can. I thought I could. I thought I could.*

That was enough thinking. The time had come for action. Everything had to be ripped apart before it could be put back together again.

Darcy turned up the sound on her portable tape deck. While the "1812 Overture" blasted energetically, she rolled up the sleeves of her baggy YALE-logo sweatshirt and attacked the mess. She plunked a stack of files into a cardboard box, taped it closed and wrote "File A–C" on the lid.

In time with the music, she swooped again. More files disappeared into a box.

Another swoop. Art books nestled in cardboard.

Another. She hefted a stack of *Forbes* magazines.

The classical music clicked to silence, and Darcy dropped the magazines in a fan.

Her beautiful, blonde cousin, Paula Nordstrom, lifted her manicured fingers from the tape player and gestured dismissively. "I told you so, darling. This is a disaster."

"Not really. It's organized. This pile is accounting work. This is research. This is—"

"Moving your office is such a dumb idea. Especially now in this slushy weather."

"But January is the perfect season for a brilliant new start," Darcy protested. "Besides, I've already paid my lease on the new office, and I'm going."

"Why? Darling, this is your family home, and there's more than enough space, not to mention that it's rent free."

"That depends," Darcy said, "upon your definition of free."

The mental energy of trying to maintain an office in the eccentric atmosphere of the Conway family mansion was an immeasureable expenditure, one that Darcy could no longer afford. She simply could not justify time away from her work to brew a pot of peppermint tea for Great-Aunt Louisa. Or to rewind Mama's aerobics videotape. Or to correct the grammar on Poppa's latest biographical study of Darcy's great-grandfather—"Lucky Jim" Conway, the man who brought railroads to Chicago.

"I'm twenty-eight years old," Darcy said. "It's high time I left home."

"You've left before," her cousin chided. "And it wasn't exactly a raging success."

"This time is different. I'm not running to some man. This time I'm moving for myself, for my own precious sanity."

"Really, Darcy." Paula perched on a worn Queen Anne chair. "At least hire a secretary to do this drab work."

"I intend to. Just as soon as I'm settled." Darcy brushed the dust from her Levis. "I'll bet you think I forgot the GCC luncheon today."

"Why would I think that? The other board members of Greater Chicago Charities will be thrilled that you've chosen to illustrate the plight of the refugee in your choice of attire."

"Obviously, I'm not going."

"Obviously." Paula crossed one Gucci boot-clad ankle over the other "I hope you'll at least change the style of your office furniture. Something Mies van der Rohe?"

"Simple and classic," Darcy agreed. "But I'm afraid my bank balance indicates discount Scandinavian until I have a few more solid investors in my pocket."

From down the hallway, they heard the high pitched squeak of Great-Aunt Louisa. "Yoo hoo, Darcy? You have a visitor."

Auntie Lou, as she was known to the legions of Conway cousins, bustled—she always bustled—into the room. "Oh my, Darcy. You aren't prepared for guests. Well, I'll just tell Mr. Jonathan Hillcroft that you aren't receiving."

"Hillcroft?" Paula gasped. "*The* Jonathan Hillcroft?"

"Do I know him?" Auntie Lou asked with a nervous flutter. "Hillcroft? Oh dear, but I've never heard of his family."

"You've got to be kidding," Paula said, rising

and homing toward the door like a swallow returning to Capistrano. "He's a billionaire, Auntie Lou, rich as Midas but a little on the reclusive side. The newspapers call him 'the Howard Hughes of the Baby Boom Generation.' I can't believe he's here. This man has got to be *the* most eligible bachelor in the world."

"Paula," Darcy stepped forward to catch her cousin's elbow. "I'm sure the man didn't come here looking for a date. If he's here on business, I don't want you crawling all over him. This is not the Conway Singles Club."

"It is now," she returned, shaking free and wafting down the hallway toward the front parlor. "I'll entertain the mysterious Mr. H. while you get changed."

Darcy paused in the doorway, trying to decide whether or not she should dash upstairs and make herself presentable. "Auntie Lou, did Mr. Hillcroft mention why he came to visit?"

"He was very polite, dear."

"Did he say this was about business?"

"Oh my, Darcy. I can't remember something like that."

Of course not. Darcy suppressed a sigh. It would be such a relief to hire a decent secretary/receptionist.

She propped herself against the door frame and wrinkled her brow. This timing truly was horrendous. Hillcroft could be the investor she needed for her business to really fly, and she couldn't afford to blow this first meeting.

To change or not to change, that was the question. If Hillcroft was really a retiring recluse, she dared not leave him too long with her cousin. Paula's aggressive sensuality turned brash men into tongue-tied lumps of quivering desire. On the other hand, Darcy's disheveled appearance didn't exactly inspire confidence in her business skills.

Would he understand? She scanned her memory for information about Hillcroft. Supposedly, he'd sold a $3 million home for a tenth of its value when reporters learned its location. He bought his own telephone service to protect his private number. The only public event he'd attended in recent years was a masked ball. Of course, that was only gossip, the tabloid data.

From more reliable sources, Darcy remembered his net worth was over $1.4 billion, right up there with the Gettys and the Hunts and the Rockefellers. Hillcroft's self-generated money initially came from real estate, then oil, then computers. His current tactics included corporate raids where he'd bought out floundering companies and turned them into profitable mega-bucks industries.

Was he an eccentric? Or a financial genius with a penchant for privacy? There was only one way to find out; she had to meet him, to shake his hand and look him in the eye.

Darcy smoothed her sweatshirt. Hopefully, this

self-made billionaire was perceptive enough to look past her grubby clothes to the professional woman inside.

She popped into the front parlor in time to see her cousin grasp the arm of a tall, unsmiling man with neatly trimmed sandy brown hair. He was quite elegant. His shoes were spotless though the residue of snow outside slopped on everyone else's feet. The Windsor knot in his striped silk tie was impeccable, and his navy blue suit was expensively tailored. He looked like he'd stepped off the pages of *GQ*.

Calculated perfection, Darcy thought, and his reserved manner seemed to match.

Despite his coolness, Paula coiled herself around him as she pointed out the oil portrait above the mantle. "This was my great-great-uncle," she exclaimed, breathily. "Lucky Jim Conway, the man who founded the family fortunes. That was back in the early 1900's, Jonathan, when railroads were king."

"Yes, I know," he replied, stiffly courteous. "My family was also in the railroad business."

"Oh," Paula exclaimed as if he'd made a scintillating comment. "I wasn't aware of that. Were you the competition?"

"Not unless you consider a switchman and two conductors to be in the same league as Lucky Jim."

For a supposed recluse, Darcy thought he handled Paula's blatant attentions quite well. Perhaps the reports of his reclusiveness were caused by what was perceived as an aloof, distant attitude. If he'd been born wealthy, the media would have called him a snob, but Hillcroft's fortune had been made in less than ten years. He was as *nouveau riche* as they came.

She cleared her throat. "Mr. Hillcroft? I'm Darcy Conway."

He disengaged from Paula, crossed the parlor with wide strides and formally extended his hand. "Thank you for seeing me without an appointment. My secretary did attempt to contact you."

"Yes, well, I haven't checked my phone messages . . ." It wouldn't do a darn bit of good to protest that she was usually organized and efficient. Her voice trailed to a disconcerted mutter. ". . . not since noon yesterday."

Confronted with all this self-assured, male perfection, Darcy felt like an idiot. She should have changed into her Halston suit to face his daunting poise and the bemused look in his thickly lashed gray eyes.

Too late now. She braced herself, making the best of a ludicrous situation, and gave his hand a swift, firm shake.

"Darcy, darling," Paula interrupted. "Why don't you go change? I'll keep Jonathan occupied in the meantime."

"Ms. Conway looks fine to me," he said. "And I am in a bit of a hurry. Please excuse us, Paula. Your office, Ms. Conway?"

"My office—" Darcy hesitated. What would he think when he saw her office? "My office is down the hall."

Stiff upper lip, she told herself as she led the way. Don't apologize. Don't explain. And never let them see you sweat.

Halfway down the hall, a door swung open and Darcy's father stuck his head into the hall. He'd moved so abruptly that his gold-frame reading glasses flew off the end of his nose. "What's going on out here?"

"Nothing, Poppa."

"A man can't get a lick of work done in this house. Not a lick." He grabbed his glasses and slammed the door.

Auntie Lou bustled past them, glanced at Jonathan and mumbled to herself, "Hillcroft? I knew a Hill family in Boston. Or was it Hale?"

Darcy directed the mysterious billionaire into her office and closed the door. With the air of someone who always operated in chaos, she climbed over boxes to the swivel chair behind her desk and sat. She gestured to the Queen Anne chair, the only other vacant surface in the room. "Won't you sit down?"

As he picked his way through the obstacle course and lowered his tall, lean frame into the chair, he stated the obvious. "I've come at an inconvenient time, haven't I?"

"Oh, no," she sardonically returned, as she poked a pink silk dahlia into her pen holder. "This is the latest thing in office decor—the ransacked look. It's designed to discourage the theft of corporate secrets."

"Might catch on," he said.

"I'm told the Pentagon is considering it. Ransacked is better than a shredder for hiding documents."

When he finally let loose with a grin, the whole aspect of his appearance changed from brooding formality to a devilish warmth. His smile brought out dimples in his cheeks and emphasized the strong line of his clean shaven jaw.

When he caught her gaze, Darcy understood the charisma of this self-made man. The faceted grey of his irises twinkled hypnotically.

To regain her poise, she had to look away, fumbling through her half-emptied desk drawers to find a lined yellow legal pad and a pencil. Back to business. "How may I help you, Mr. Hillcroft?"

"I want you to come to Aspen on Friday."

"The ski resort in Colorado?" Taken aback, her mind reeled. She loved skiing. A trip to Aspen sounded heavenly.

Immediately, she squelched the idea. How would she get her offices moved, the phones installed, the secretary hired if she was indulging in a schuss down Aspen slopes?

"I will, of course, reimburse you for plane tickets and three days' lodgings," he assured her. "I am interested in appraisals, mainly."

Darcy knew to tread lightly at this point. Her business, Original Property Brokers, raised loan monies using special, appraised items as collateral. Since most of her clients were wealthy individuals in reduced circumstances, Darcy knew the importance of tact. "What sort of objects did you wish to have appraised?"

"A little of this, little of that."

His evasiveness was typical of people who were about to put their priceless treasures on the line. Yet Darcy found it inconceivable that Jonathan Hillcroft was in financial straits. Her business required her to keep abreast of developments in the financial community, and she surely would have heard if Hillcroft were in difficulty. Besides, the man positively radiated confidence, and he'd offered to pay for transportation and lodging. That certainly didn't seem like someone who was short of cash.

On the other hand, she reminded herself, things weren't always as they seemed. Her own family exemplified a supposedly wealthy clan that verged perpetually on the brink of bankruptcy.

If Hillcroft were in sudden need of liquidity, he was probably embarrassed, and it wouldn't be the first time she'd dealt with a tycoon. "I need to know more about the proposed transaction," she said. "Could you give me an idea of the value of the items you wish to have appraised? A ballpark figure?"

"I'd rather not," he said. Another smile teased the corner of his lips. "I'm not in need of a loan, Ms. Conway."

"Then I don't understand why you've come to see

me. My business arranges financing against the worth of special properties, artworks, antiques, and so forth."

"I'm aware of that. My reason for contacting you is that I want your expert opinion. I've recently acquired several items, and I need to know if they're authentic."

Darcy was perplexed. "But I'm not an acknowledged expert. I have no credentials."

Though she was usually able to spot a fake, Darcy relied on a stable of museum personnel, jewelers, and art experts to document worth and authenticity. Her expertise was an ability to judge human character, to weed out the conmen from those who truly had something of value to offer.

She trained her expert eye upon Jonathan Hillcroft. Not a conman, she thought, but he wasn't being one hundred percent sincere with her, either. There was a hidden agenda that intrigued her. "Why are you really inviting me to Aspen?"

"I'd rather not explain." He glanced at his Rolex wristwatch. "I'm willing to pay for your time. Two thousand per diem?"

"Two thousand dollars?"

"I'm not talking yen, pesos, or pounds."

Two thousand dollars a day to visit Aspen? Talk about your all-expenses paid vacations!

Darcy's usual fee for arranging a loan was one percent of the package, an amount that could range in the tens of thousands of dollars. However, she was also accustomed to expending her time and efforts for nothing—appraising a Picasso that turned out to be fake or having a client with cold feet or courting a venture capitalist whose greatest venture was the purchase of a business card. Hillcroft's deal was guaranteed, money in the bank. Her imagination indulged in glittering visions of ski slopes.

"Will I see you on Friday?" he asked.

"That will be quite satisfactory. I'll plan to arrive on Thursday night."

"Fine. Your reservations will be made at the Glacier Lodge. Do you ski?"

"Yes." She quickly added, "But I don't have time right now for a skiing vacation."

"Perhaps we can meet on the slopes."

"If you'd prefer," she said, recalling the cardinal rule of business: The customer is always right. Besides, it would be downright inefficient not to take advantage of the snow.

Her pencil hovered over a scrap of paper. "When and where shall we meet?"

"I'll contact you there." His grin was apologetic. "I try never to give precise appointments. To avoid publicity."

"I understand," she said. Was this a glimpse of the famous reclusive behavior? If so, she didn't find it odd at all. Rather his precautions seemed sensible. "And I promise not to send out invitations."

"I know, Darcy, your reputation for discrete consultation precedes you. Nonetheless, there are always extenuating possibilities, and I cherish the privacy I've been able to establish in Aspen."

Cherished privacy, she repeated to herself, what a lovely turn of phrase. Though he probably defined privacy as a dark, snowy night and a hot buttered rum before a blazing fire, she also cherished her moments of solitude. That was, in fact, one of the main reasons she wanted to move from the family home into her own apartment near her new office—a quiet place of her own where she could sit up all night reading or writing letters or finishing that needlepoint pillow she'd started four Christmases ago. A peaceful atmosphere without interruption.

She blinked away the mental image and said, "I'll wait for your message."

"Then it's settled." He took a flat wallet from the pocket of his suitcoat and dealt out six one thousand dollar bills. While Darcy gaped, he placed the cash amid the chaos of her desktop. "Will three days advance be sufficient?"

"Do you always carry that much cash?"

"A bad habit," he agreed.

"Let me find you a receipt," she said, leaving her desk and diving toward a cardboard box marked: "Acct."

"It's not necessary." He stepped over a stack of magazines, came around her desk, and extended his hand. "I assume that the Conway family is accustomed to doing business with a gentleman's handshake."

"Or a gentlewoman's," she said, taking his hand.

She was both pleased and surprised when her usually firm, businesslike grip melted in his grasp, sending warmth from her fingertips throughout her body. His handshake gave new meaning to the phrase "pressing the flesh," creating a shocking desire in Darcy to press more of herself against him.

But this didn't make sense. Their first handshake in the parlor had been a crisp introduction; this was different, marvelously different. Here, in the privacy of her disarrayed office, there was a sense of intimacy between them, as if they shared a very special secret.

"Thank you, Darcy." His gaze rested warmly on her face, caressing her lips and her eyelashes. "For trusting me."

"Six thousand dollars buys a lot of trust."

"You can't comprehend how important this is to me. With your help, I hope to fulfill a life-long dream."

When he ended the handclasp and slipped on a pair of dark glasses, she felt like the sun had gone behind a cloud.

Vaguely, she remembered ten thousand professional questions she ought to be asking: What sort of item did he need verified? Had he already purchased said items? Was he interested in precise monetary value? Why had he contacted her?

"Thank you," he murmured. "I've enjoyed doing business with one of Lucky Jim Conway's descendants."

TWO

On Friday morning in Aspen, the chairlift bumped against the back of Darcy's legs, and she automatically bent her knees. With a whoosh, she was swept off her feet. Her white Head skis dangled above the glittering, snow-covered terrain.

Her companion on the chairlift was Jonathan Hillcroft.

She hadn't known what to expect when she met him. Would the intriguing sense of intimacy resurface? Or would he be businesslike, cold, and formal? Jonathan completely defeated her speculations by producing yet another persona. The face he wore in Aspen was friendly, laughing, and easygoing. But he showed absolutely no awareness of her as a woman.

They'd jostled each other in the chairlift line. He hadn't offered to help her with her skis. He hadn't

23

even fed her breakfast. But Darcy didn't complain. She rather liked this version, and she was far more comfortable with a male friend than a lover. With everything else going on in her life, Darcy was decidedly *not* looking for a man.

"Paula's going to kill me," she said cheerfully.

"Paula, your secretary?" Jonathan pushed his ski goggles back on his forehead and raised his eyebrows. "Why do I find Paula as a secretary hard to believe?"

"Because Paula's never worked a day in her life and it shows. More than anyone in my family, Paula is the essence of beautiful idleness." Darcy wondered if he was attracted to Paula. Most men were. "Of course, she's not really a secretary despite what she told you, and I hasten to add that I was not the one who informed her about this trip to Aspen."

"Guilty. The indiscretion was mine. She caught me unawares on the veranda of your house in Chicago." He gave Darcy one of those devastating grins. "Why is she going to kill you?"

"Because when I got the wake-up call this morning with your message to meet for breakfast, I promised that we would wait for her in the lodge."

"It wasn't your fault," he said. "I was the one who dragged you out to the slopes."

"Paula will never believe that, but I'm glad you did." Darcy tentatively shifted her weight, acclimating herself to the odd sensation of being suspended in air. "We were almost first in the lift line and we still had to wait seventeen minutes."

"Worked out well, but I wasn't thinking of the wait."

"I know," she said. "I couldn't help noticing the guy with the camera. Is he after you for an interview?"

"Not really. He's after the mythical Jonathan Hill-croft, who's carrying on the Howard Hughes tradition of weird recluse with five inch long toenails and fetishes about sanitation."

She looked at him and laughed. This handsome, athletic man was anything but a hermit. Clad in black from the top of his ski cap to the toes of his shiny Lange boots, he radiated health and energy. "I've heard," she said in a conspirator's tone, "that you always wear a mask in public."

"That's tame," he said. "There have been stories that I've fathered an alien child, that I drink lamb's blood, and live in a flotation tank. I guess the reporters don't want to believe that I'm a boring, ordinary guy."

She nodded. Just an ordinary guy. With a bank balance that could pay off the national debt.

Darcy filled her lungs with clean, cold air. The icy winds through the pines nipped her cheeks to a crimson glow, and she peered over her shoulder at the glacial white mountains surrounding them. They were on their way to the top of the world. The pinnacle.

A shiver of anticipation went through her. What a

marvelous day! In her opinion, life didn't get much better than this. She was outdoors, invigorated and snuggly warm in insulated snow pants, parka, and heavy leather gloves. Her outfit was much like Jonathan's except her color was lavender with a pale blue yoke on her parka.

"Fantastic weather," she said. Her voice hung frozen in the air, an echo of misty vapor.

"Glad you approve. I arranged the blue skies just for you. And precisely three inches of fresh powder snow."

She glanced at the slopes where early morning skiers soared across moguls, etching criss-cross tracks across the panorama of January snow. "I wish I could stay longer."

"Did you get your office moved?"

"Moved, but not unpacked. I do, however, have the phones connected and a secretary hired. She'll keep in touch with me if anything important comes up." The chairlift jolted to a halt, and Darcy held tight to the bar between them. "Since neither of us is going anywhere, this might be a good time to ask you about our business. Tell me about the items you wish to have appraised."

"I'd rather show you."

"It's up to you," she said with a shrug. "But I am curious. Can you at least tell me the purpose of this appraisal?"

"I'm thinking of a trade. There's something very special that I wish to acquire. Something that money can't buy. Your expertise will help me decide what to offer in exchange.''

''Something beyond price,'' she mused. ''An artwork?''

''To me it's art. I don't suppose the rest of the world would agree.''

''A building? Or a piece of property?''

''No.'' He shook his head.

The chairlift started up again, and they continued their ascent. Darcy was fascinated by Hillcroft's plan and professionally curious. When Jonathan Hillcroft intended to purchase or trade for something, his action was significant, capable of causing tidal waves in the financial community.

She remembered his penchant for corporate raids and wondered. Certainly, he was not interested in acquiring Original Property Brokers. Darcy's company was too much an extension of her own personality to be of general interest. ''Why me?''

''My market research shows you're the best source.''

''Market research?'' She chuckled. ''I've always thought that was a fancy term for gossip: Who's buying what? Why? Where?''

''You're absolutely right. It's all about learning to be in the right place at the right time.''

''Can you at least tell me who owns this treasured thing?''

''That's part of my problem. Technically, the ownership is convoluted. I'm going to have to convince at least three different people to relinquish their claim."

"An inheritance problem?"

"You've guessed it."

Her business frequently brought her into contact with situations involving a complicated estate where the deceased had not been crystal clear in his or her Last Will and Testament. She thoroughly sympathized with Jonathan's problem—dealing with one heir was difficult, trying to appease three could be impossible.

"Tell me about the family," she said.

"I don't know them personally, but I've heard that they can be very determined, very involved in their own special interests."

"I understand. When you say 'determined' you mean stubborn. 'Special interests' means eccentric hobbies."

"A lethal combination," he agreed. "And I need to meet with them on a calm, sensible basis."

She considered. This expenses-paid ski trip to Aspen was beginning to make sense. Jonathan did not require her services as an appraiser. Instead, he wanted her to provide an introduction to one of the old, wealthy, oddball families.

"Very clever," she complimented him. "You want me to negotiate with somebody's maiden aunt who won't meet with you. But would gladly accept an invitation to afternoon tea from Lucky Jim Conway's great-granddaughter."

"Bingo. But I also do have some items to appraise."

"Sure you do," she said, disbelievingly. "You brought me here under false pretenses, Jonathan. My maidenly sensibilities really ought to be offended."

"But they're not."

"I'm too much of a practical businesswoman to be coy. The only news that causes me to swoon is the Dow Jones average. And I understand your problem completely. Eccentric families can be an incredible pain in the neck. I doubt that anyone knows that better than I do."

His leather glove touched her thigh, sending an unwanted tremor through her body. Darcy recoiled, prudently suppressing feelings that were surely inappropriate. "What, Jonathan?"

"You're not angry with me, are you?"

"Of course not. I approve of your plan. You'll save yourself a lot of idiotic social climbing by letting me act as your ally. Although I don't quite understand why you didn't present this plan to me in the first place. And why bring me all the way to Aspen?"

"I wanted to see you again," he said.

Pow! Sparkling snowflakes exploded in her brain. He wanted to see her again. "Why?"

"I ascribe to the old-fashioned way of doing business," he said. "You can't really trust an associate unless you've skied with them."

Darcy forced her excitement to settle. He wasn't

talking about a desire for her, simply a manner of wheeling and dealing. "Or played golf with them. Or tennis."

"Exactly." He squinted up toward the summit. "Almost there. How well do you ski?"

"I'm better than my two brothers and my sister, but that's not saying much. Let's take the easy slopes."

"Not the beginner trails?" he scoffed.

"Intermediate," she said as the lift bucked and stopped. "And you're not going to change the subject. Who is this oddball family?"

"I'd rather not say. Not yet."

His hesitation was interesting. Though he'd hired a Conway to squeeze into the confidence of some upper-upper crust family, Jonathan didn't quite trust her. Not that she blamed him for that reluctance. She was often amazed at the silliness that had emerged from the Conway genetic pool. Many of her relatives seemed to have been bred for the sole purpose of finding new and more expensive pleasures.

Of all the clan, Darcy was the only one who had inherited her great-grandfather's talent for tough entrepreneurial endeavor. Even that wasn't a comparison she liked to dwell upon.

Though Lucky Jim had amassed a fortune during the early days of railroads, his methods were often less than honest. The elderly great-aunts and cousins who still remembered him told gory tales of his sharklike greed and viciousness. Then they would nod toward Darcy and thank the heavens that somebody was carrying on the Conway tradition.

The chairlift bumped to life, and Darcy raised the tips of her skis, preparing to dismount. "Come on, Jonathan," she urged. "Tell me who they are."

"Go to your right when you get off the chair," he instructed.

"Are they from Chicago?" She lowered her skis and coasted smoothly down the incline from the chairlift. After checking her bindings and firmly grasping her ski poles, Darcy pulled up curtly beside him. "Jonathan—who?"

"In case we get separated, take the first left, then just follow the markings for the Intermediate trail." Before he lowered his goggles into place, he winked. "I'll satisfy your curiosity, Darcy, when we reach the bottom."

He took two gliding steps and zoomed away from her.

Her ski poles dug into the crust with a light crunch, and she took off. A fine spray of crystalline powder swirled in her wake. Her flawless christie turns propelled her over the moguls, and she traversed with feet together and skis in a classic parallel. The chill wind whipped against her face, but the exhilaration of downhill speed warmed her.

Breathless, she halted. Where had Jonathan disappeared to? She'd been concentrating so hard on her own skiing that she hadn't been watching for him. She shrugged. Undoubtedly, he was an expert skier and was already three-quarters of the way down the slope.

No reason for him to wait, she thought. It wasn't like she was helpless. Though unfamiliar with the Aspen slopes, she was perfectly capable of making it down the mountain on her own steam. She certainly wasn't a beginner like Paula. Darcy's jaw tightened. He would have waited for Paula, she thought.

Her pace was relaxed as she dipped and glided from one snow field to another. Yet, a vague anxiety flitted across her mental horizon. Though Jonathan's reluctance to name the eccentric family disconcerted her, she was more worried about the strange excitement she experienced in his presence. When he innocently touched her or when their eyes met, her response bordered on lust. Not exactly lust, she corrected herself. Raw biological desire would have been easier for her to handle than this odd sort of romanticism. Fantasies were innate for most Conways, but she generally managed to control herself.

She aimed her ski tips at a narrow trail marked "Intermediate" and pushed off at a smooth pace, enjoying the shadowed serenity of the towering, snow-laden pines on either side. A chattering schuss came from behind her, a sound more felt than heard, and a shout. What had the other skier said? On your right? Or left?

She glanced over her shoulder in time to see a black-clad figure rising from a speed skier's crouch.

He seemed to be on her right and she moved to the left—just as he did.

The impact was so sudden that she didn't have time to scream. She felt no pain, only surprise that her gentle cruise had turned into a rolling snowball descent. Arms and legs and skis tangled together as they crashed out of the tunnel of trees onto a wider slope.

Darcy was face down in a snowbank with the downhill racer sprawled atop her lower body. His weight immobilized her, but she lifted her head in time to see one of her skis caroom down the hill.

"Are you all right?" he asked.

"Jonathan!" It figured. All day long he'd been knocking her over-active imagination for a loop, it was only appropriate that he should physically bowl her over as well.

"Darcy, are you all right?"

She swallowed a mouthful of snow. "I've been better."

"I'm sorry. But you did jump into my path."

"Jump?" she snapped. "I didn't jump anywhere. If you hadn't been roaring down this skinny trail like the Cannonball Express . . ."

He laughed. "Trust a Conway to compare a ski slope to a locomotive."

"This isn't funny. What were you trying to do?"

"I was looking for you. You went right instead of left on the first slope, and I've been looking for you ever since. That's why I was going so fast."

"Don't blame your negligence on me," she said, irritably. "Now that there's no need to rush, maybe you could get off me."

"I'll try." He lifted himself on his forearms and immediately sank in the soft snow, finally floundering to a position beside her. "Did you know you were missing a ski?"

"Yes," she hissed.

"I'm really sorry." His gloved hand brushed a lock of her dark hair from her face, and Darcy found herself staring into his compelling hazel grey eyes. His lashes were spikey wet from the snow bath and his tanned cheeks were ruddy. "Are you sure you're okay?"

"How can I be sure? I couldn't move while you were on top of me."

"Is that any way to talk after I've literally swept you off your feet?" His raised eyebrows hinted that he commonly heard a more positive response from the women who lay beneath him. "Not that this is my idea of a great seduction," he added.

Darcy rolled her eyes. Men! Only a male could make sexual innuendos while flat on his back in a snowbank. But she felt an incongruous burst of trembling deep inside. Did he mean it? A seduction?

She flexed her knees cautiously and wiggled her ankles. There was a slight soreness, but everything seemed to be in working order. Probable bruises, she thought, but no broken bones. When she struggled to a sitting position, however, she cried out.

"What's the matter? Are you hurt?"

"Damn." Her mouth filled with the acrid taste of disappointment and pain. "It's my left wrist."

"Let me see." He hovered over her on his hands and knees. "Don't worry, Darcy. I learned basic first aid with the ski patrol. I won't make it worse. Can you move your fingers?"

She could. Carefully, she removed her leather glove. The wrist wasn't broken, but swelling had already started.

"Probably a sprain," he diagnosed. His grey eyes softened. "God, I'm sorry."

He really did look sorry. And handsome and self-assured, she irrelevantly observed. Even with the dark traces of his morning beard unshaven, Jonathan qualified as a sandy-haired, square-jawed species of Aspen Adonis. Not that it made the tiniest bit of difference, she reminded herself as she looked away from him. Her injury was the same whether she'd collided with a geek or a hunk.

"Might be a hairline fracture," he said, scrambling to gather his ski gear. "You'll need X-rays. If it's a sprain, it should be packed in ice to lessen the swelling."

She glanced around her at the wide vista of snow. Descending the mountain to apply ice to her wrist seemed absurdly like "water, water everywhere, and not a drop to drink."

"I know what you're thinking," he said. "And you can forget it. Self-treatment is never a good idea when you can get to a doctor. Frostbite is a poor alternative to an ice pack. Now, let's go."

"Very sensible," she agreed. "But forgive me if I'm not thrilled to bits about a long, steep walk."

"Who said anything about walking? I'll carry you."

"Carry me?" Her voice frosted with sarcasm. "No thanks. I've already had one example of your skiing prowess."

"You're not scared of me, are you?"

"Of course not."

"Then let's drop the Ice Princess routine."

Scared? She clenched her jaw. Ice Princess? It wasn't the first time she'd been accused of being cold, but it *was* the most inappropriate. She was prudent, but not a prude; unfortunately, not where Jonathan was concerned.

He fastened her poles and ski slantwise across his back with the belt on his parka, bent his knees and slipped one arm beneath her knees and one around her back. "I'll be careful."

Her attempt to wriggle away from him resulted in a shooting pain from her left wrist. She tensed as she felt herself being lifted, scooped into his arms. Defenseless and vulnerable, she concentrated on control. She didn't want to cry. She didn't want to embarrass herself. "I don't want to be carried."

"We're close to the bottom," he assured her. "If I skied down to notify the ski patrol, they'd have to come all the way from the top towing the litter. It would take over an hour.''

"If we're that close, I'd rather take my chances and walk. It's my arm that's sprained, not my leg. Please put me down.''

"Nope." He tightened his grasp around her knees and upper body. "You could make your injury worse if you fell again.''

"I didn't fall. I was pushed." Under her breath, she added, "I happened to be in the right place at the wrong time.''

"Relax, Darcy. Let me take care of you.''

In a wide Vee snow plow, he traversed the slope. Though she had to admit that his progress was slow and careful, she hated being carried. She didn't even like to ride in a car when someone else was driving. Her independent nature was well known among family and friends, and they turned to her for help. Not the other way around.

"Hang on, Darcy. We're almost there," Jonathan assured.

Almost where? Her wrist was beginning to throb. Offering a little prayer to whatever gods reigned over injured skiers, she gritted her teeth and leaned against him.

Through his black parka, she felt a reassuring firmness. The sinewed arms that held her must be terrifically strong, she thought. Though she was slim, her height was five feet six inches, and she was considerably heavier than a goose down pillow. His legs must be equally powerful to support the strain of her extra weight. He wasn't even breathing hard.

Damn. Darcy tensed. She knew she was perilously close to making a fool out of herself with Jonathan, betraying this crazy longing. Why did he have to be so heart-breakingly masculine?

"I'll come back for your ski," he promised. "And you're coming to my place after you've been treated."

"Not necessary. Our rooms at the Glacier Lodge are more than adequate, and if I need someone to look after me, Paula's there."

"Ah yes, the lovely Paula."

Darcy felt a pinprick of anger. Of course he would remember Paula as being lovely. Just as he would think of her as an Ice Princess.

He jolted over a bump and stopped. "Do you trust me to get to the bottom without dropping you?"

"I guess so."

"Then would you please relax. I feel like I'm carrying a stick woman."

He had no idea what he was asking. Half the day she had been fighting the desire to fall into his arms, to throw herself mindlessly at his gorgeous body.

"Please, Darcy. It's difficult to carry you when you're so stiff. Relax."

With a sigh, she let down the barriers she'd constructed to keep her emotions at a safe distance. She nestled against his chest, releasing the tension from her limbs and making herself limp as a kitten. "Is this better?"

"Much."

The morning temperature in Aspen, Colorado, couldn't have been much above freezing, but Darcy was warm all over. This was the closest she had been to a man in a long time, near enough to smell his toasty aroma, to hear his heartbeat.

She closed her eyes. There was nothing she could do for herself in this suspended position. She accepted it, accepted him. Her fate was in his hands. In his arms. With the purity of snow all around her, Darcy somehow knew she was safe.

THREE

With her left wrist secured in a temporary splint, Darcy stared at the glowing embers of the fire Jonathan had built before he left. She could have tossed on another log one-handed, but she was warm enough without the fire.

She was, in fact, hot with anger and frustration. Not only had her weekend of skiing been ruined, but her idiotic, unfounded attraction to Jonathan had accelerated. And now he'd disappeared—supposedly to inform Paula about her injury.

For the twentieth time, Darcy checked her wrist watch. Jonathan had been gone for one hour and forty-nine minutes. He'd probably located her cousin long ago. They were probably standing around in the lodge admiring each other.

She took a deep breath and slowly expelled it. At

least he'd deserted her in the first-class surroundings of his private home. She glared around the living room, finding fault with the expensive furnishings. In her present mood, she would have found fault with the Sistine Chapel.

With angry satisfaction, she found the huge, brass-trimmed fireplace inefficient. The high tech chrome lamps were common, and those circular brass staircases were always difficult to climb. Though his home was spacious and well-lit with tall windows all around, she'd never understood the logic of planting eight-foot tall trees indoors. Who needs to rake in summer?

Not that Jonathan raked up after himself, she thought. He undoubtedly had a maid for this typical bachelor's pad. Someone to comb the fur robes that were draped casually over the fifteen-foot long sectional sofa, someone to vacuum the bear skin rug.

High beamed ceilings and three original oils by Fredric Remington, Wyeth, and Pollack modified her distaste, but did not change her essential impression. The decor was uniquely familiar from Chicago to Colorado: generic stud.

Though she hadn't climbed the fragile-looking staircase to explore the upper floor, she suspected that the second level would be devoted to a hedonistic set of bedrooms, probably with round, rotating beds and mirrors on the ceiling.

He and Paula deserved each other.

Almost as though she'd been heard by the north

wind, the mahogany door to the condominium swung open, and her cousin breezed inside. Her sleek blonde hair fluffed against a chic silver fox jacket. "Oh, Darcy," she wailed as she rushed across the room. "Are you all right?"

"On a scale of one to ten, I'm five."

"You don't look bad at all," Paula accused.

"Sorry to disappoint you. Next time, I'll try for a concussion and three broken limbs."

Paula went to the fireplace, yanked off her mittens and held her hands out to the dying flames. "Congratulations, darling. You've gotten inside Jonathan's home. Talk about the luck of the Irish!"

"Aren't you forgetting something?" Darcy asked as she pointed to the splint on her left forearm.

"It's not serious, is it?"

"It's enough to keep me off the slopes."

"A small sacrifice," Paula said as she scrutinized the signature on the Pollack. "I think you and Jonathan can find several pleasurable alternatives to skiing."

"Me and Jonathan? Guess again. He thinks I'm some kind of combination sidekick and Ice Princess."

"That's hardly the case. The man is passionate about you." Her expression was critical. "I know you've been out of circulation for a while, but don't blow this, Darcy."

"I have no idea what you're talking about," she said, while one of those annoying tingles of excitement went through her. Paula's judgments about men were generally accurate. "In any case, it doesn't matter one way or the other. I'm not interested in any kind of involvement."

"You've found one anyway. On the way over here, all he could talk about was you. Darcy this and Darcy that. What does Darcy like? Is Darcy seeing anyone special right now? I tell you, lovey, it was insulting. I mean, here I was in my best fur, looking positively cuddly, and he kept talking about you."

"Probably a smoke screen," she said, suppressing her delight. "He must have been pumping you for information, trying to figure out if I intended to sue him."

Darcy shifted on the sofa. Jonathan's interest in her was gratifying. She remembered the strength in his arms as he carried her down the slopes, how he'd rested his hand possessively on her shoulder while the ski patrol doctor examined her sprained wrist. There was a sheer animal appeal to the man that could not be denied.

Paula flounced up the two stairs to the kitchen level and pronounced it a disaster area. "Just look at this mess! Dishes and pans and—ah ha, another similarity between you and Jonathan in whom you are not interested—TV dinner cartons. You are obviously made for each other. Neither of you can cook."

"Mutual starvation, a swell basis for a relationship," Darcy said sardonically. "I really don't think you should be going through the man's garbage, Paula.''

"But you can learn a lot about someone from their trash. Discarded *Wall Street Journal*. Imported beer bottles. Oh dear, there's a noticeable absence of caviar tins.''

"The next thing you'll be doing is reading his mail.''

"I would,'' she shamelessly confirmed, "but I don't see any. Wait, here's a snapshot of Jonathan. And it looks like he's holding an antique switchman's lantern. What do you think?''

Before Paula could cross the room, Darcy waved her away. "I refuse to dignify your snooping with any speculation.''

"Come on, darling. I'm trying to be big-hearted, noble in defeat and all that. It's no secret that I set my cap for Jonathan. But he's attracted to you, and you have my blessing.'' Her tone became serious. "Give him a chance, Darcy. Not all men are like Thomas.''

Darcy was grateful for the interruption when Jonathan barged through the door, his arms piled high with firewood. She didn't want to discuss her live-in experience with Thomas O'Bannion. Though their affair ended two years ago, her own blind stupidity still infuriated her. She'd been so gullible, and Thomas had used her, played her for a fool.

As far as Darcy was concerned, Thomas was history. Still, she shrewdly reminded herself, one can learn valuable lessons from history. Darcy would never allow herself to be used again.

Jonathan deposited the firewood in a brass coal hod. "How's the wrist?"

"I'm not ready for a rousing game of Ping-Pong, but it doesn't hurt unless I move it."

"Could you manage to hoist a cup of Irish coffee to your lips?"

Darcy waved with her good right hand and said, "When it comes to Irish coffee, I'm ambidexterous."

His march toward the kitchen was stopped by Paula. "Tell me where you keep the liquor and I'll mix the drinks."

"The cabinet between the dining area and the kitchen, but why don't you relax. I'd be happy to—"

"I've seen your kitchen, Jonathan," she said, pinching her tiny nose between her fingers. "Pardon me if I don't want to catch trichinosis from an unwashed mug."

"Trichinosis comes from pork," he informed her without apology.

"That's a charming bit of information, darling. With your housekeeping habits, you must be an expert on food poisoning."

As she flounced toward the liquor cabinet, he returned to tend the fire, expertly stacking logs and fanning the flame. With studied casualness, he tossed a question over his shoulder to Darcy. "Paula tells me you're Irish."

"Twice Irish. Lucky Jim and his wife were immigrants from County Cork. But that was a couple of generations back."

"You look like an Irish lassie," he persisted. "With your black hair and blue eyes. Do you mean to tell me that your favorite color isn't green?"

Before Darcy could refute his stereotyping, Paula intervened. "The only thing Irish about Darcy is her temper. In all other aspects, she's more like her mother's side of the family—the cold-blooded Swedes. Darcy is fully capable of flash-freezing with one glance."

Darcy gave a low, exasperated growl, and Paula retreated back to the kitchen. "See what I mean?" she said.

He left the now blazing fire and faced her. "Tell me your family revelations about the legendary Lucky Jim Conway."

She glanced up abruptly. "Is this idle curiosity?"

"Far from idle. I'm really interested."

Darcy cringed. In her experience, people who were interested in Lucky Jim generally had an ax to grind. She hoped, really hoped, that Jonathan wasn't going to tell her how Lucky Jim had evicted his widowed great-grandmother or cheated at cards and wiped out his family's fortune. Hesitantly, she asked, "Did someone in your family know someone in mine?"

"Not likely. But I wish I could go back in a time machine and meet the man who helped make Chicago into a major railroad town. Lucky Jim is one of my heroes.''

No one had ever referred to that fierce old reprobate as a hero. "You're kidding."

"Why should that shock you?" he asked.

"Let's just say that the Lucky Jim Conway Fan Club has an extremely limited membership."

"The sixteenth of June, 1902. Grand Central Station in Chicago. It was the inaugural journey of the Twentieth Century Limited, and your great-grandfather was the first to greet her. Legend has it that Lucky Jim tipped his top hat and said, 'About time.' When the conductor pointed out that the train was on schedule, Jim Conway explained that it was about time that Vanderbilt did something right." Jonathan smiled. "I've got to admire an empire builder who acknowledges the competition without admitting defeat."

Darcy listened suspiciously to his recitation, waiting for the other shoe to drop. This anecdote, featuring Lucky Jim in one of his more benevolent moods, ended at a negotiating table when her great-grandfather lied about the arrival time—a lie that provoked Vanderbilt's famed offer of "twenty dollars to every passenger for every minute late," an offer that was later modified to one dollar per hour.

Yet Jonathan said nothing more. Either he chose to be tactful or was not informed of the whole sequence of events. More likely, she thought, Jonathan the successful businessman shared the ambitious philosophies of Lucky Jim Conway—ethics that fell slightly short of bloodthirsty. "Do you consider yourself and Lucky Jim to be kindred spirits?"

"Not really. My guess is that Jim grabbed life with both hands, took what he wanted, seized the moment. I'm more of a patient plotter."

She tried to read his expression. The high cheekbones and cleft chin suggested a hardness. His black ski clothes reminded her of the bad guy in a Western movie who tied the heroine to the railroad tracks. Yet his smile was easygoing, and his grey eyes offered unconditional friendliness.

If only she knew what to expect from him. He had the advantage of being familiar with her family history, while she knew very little about him. And that felt decidedly odd.

In her work, the situation was usually reversed. She knew the intimate secrets of those who applied for her special kind of loan service. Now the shoe was on the other foot, and she didn't particularly like the fit.

He was waiting, she realized, waiting for her to ask the next question, to set the tone for their conversation. And what could she do? Demand to see a resume? She decided to stall. Lifting her gaze to the wall of windows, she noncommittally said, "Terrific view."

Beyond a stand of winter-barren aspen trees, a downhill slope was visible, occasionally marked by the tiny, darting figures of skiers. In the distance, a panorama of snowy peaks gleamed against the clear blue sky. Darcy felt a catch in her throat. "Such wonderful snow conditions," she said. "And all I can do is sit here and look at it."

"Why don't you stay for a week?" he suggested. "Take advantage of the skiing."

"The doctor told me four to six weeks before I could ski."

"Maybe we can convince him to utilize some of that advanced orthopedic technology. An air cast or something that would immobilize your wrist and allow you to get back on the slopes in a matter of days instead of weeks."

"Really?" She brightened, then remembered another sort of mountain—the mountain of work that awaited her in her new offices. "No, I need to get back to Chicago as soon as our business is concluded."

"No time for a vacation?"

"Not for me. I'm still a struggling, little entrepreneur and I can't leave my shop untended." She couldn't resist a teasing dig. "Of course, a meglomillionaire hermit like yourself wouldn't understand."

"On the contrary. I wasn't born rich," he returned her needle. "My first million came when I was twenty-eight and I'm now thirty-eight. So, I spent roughly three-quarters of my life being broke."

"And while you were broke," she challenged, "did you take off on vacations?"

"I always had time for dreams." He shrugged. "Stay for a week?"

"No. It was terribly inefficient of me to sprain my wrist, and I can't compound that irresponsibility by ignoring my business."

"Fine, then you will depart as scheduled. In the meantime, I insist that you stay here. Paula, too."

"Not a chance," came a shout from the kitchen. "What I mean is that Darcy should stay, but I can't. I'm leaving right after we've had our coffee." She poked her head around the corner and concluded with a wink, "I have a date at two."

"Already?" Darcy teased.

"Darling, I only have a few days to make my impact on the hunks of Aspen."

Jonathan looked from Paula to Darcy. "Are you two really related?"

"Hard to believe," Darcy agreed. "But I'm closer to Paula than to my sister or my brothers. Probably because we're the same age. We went to the same boarding schools, giggled through the same parties, skinned our respective knees on the same sidewalks."

"Right next door to each other," he said. "On that oak-lined, Midwestern avenue. With the two-story, white houses and wide verandas."

There was a wistfulness in his voice that puzzled her. "Did you grow up in a similar neighborhood?"

"Not at all. My home town was ranch-style and adobe. In the Napa Valley of California where the predominant foliage is vineyard, not oak."

Paula emerged from the kitchen carrying a silver

tray with three steaming mugs of Irish coffee. "Libation," she announced.

Jonathan proposed the toast. "Let's drink to Darcy getting back on the Aspen slopes."

When they clinked mugs and drank, Jonathan caught her gaze. The depths of his eyes were as sweet as the Irish coffee and Darcy could not bring herself to look away.

"Well, well," Paula interrupted. "How was the skiing, Darcy? Before you fell."

"Incredible. It's so beautiful here. There really aren't adequate words. While I was skiing, I felt like I personally had discovered the Rocky Mountains. I was omnipotent, yet humbled at the same time."

"I know exactly what you mean," Paula commented. "I had the same idea when I walked into the Great Hall of the lodge last night and saw all those bronzed faces and broad shoulders. Which reminds me, I need to get ready for my date."

"Take the Bronco," Jonathan offered.

In a smooth move, he pulled his car keys from his pocket and held them out to Paula who swiftly accepted them. Their maneuver was too graceful to be spontaneous. Darcy raised her eyebrows and accused her friend. "You planned this."

"Guilty as charged. I'll be back before dinner. Unless my knight in shining armor decides to carry me off into the sunset."

Darcy groaned.

"Don't worry. I'll call first." Paula slipped into

her fur and sailed toward the door, offering one final word of advice before leaving. "If I were you, Darcy, I wouldn't chance dinner here. Take it from one who's inspected the kitchen: Order out."

Darcy settled back on the sofa, stretching her legs straight out on a matching ottoman. Though she recognized that Paula's motivation was blatant matchmaking, she was pleased with this turn of events. There were too many questions left unanswered between Jonathan and herself, and she meant to fill in the blanks.

But first there was an essential order of business. "Would you mind if I called the lodge and had my messages forwarded?"

"I'll take care of it," he said. "My telephone system is a bit complicated."

After he punched a series of numbers at a telephone console that was the size of an office computer and left a message at the lodge, he asked, "Don't you trust Paula's promise to return?"

"Not in the slightest," she said with a grin. "I know that glazed look she had in her eye. Either she's planning a shopping binge or a romantic fling with her knight. And I don't think she'll find a telephone on the back of his white stallion."

"That sounds a bit cynical."

"I know my cousin. She tends to get carried away."

"What about you, Darcy?"

"I've had my share of white knights," she said.

"But I've never made it past the moat and into Camelot. My knights seem to be fond of galloping around in circles."

"Must have been the wrong knights."

Though she kept her sky-blue eyes focused on the crackling fire, she knew his penetrating gaze rested upon her. She could feel the searching power, intent as a predator. Yet she wasn't uncomfortable. Instead, she was surrounded by warmth, a peaceful feeling of security.

"Paula mentioned that you're not involved with anyone right now," he said, casually taking a seat beside her on the sofa.

"Does that matter?" Her tactile senses were alerted by his nearness. Beneath her lavender turtleneck, she felt the hairs on her arms begin to prickle.

"Of course it matters. I don't care for one-night stands."

"Knight with a K?" she questioned. "I take it you're a one-damsel man."

"And very partial to Irish lassies."

Slowly, she turned her head toward him. His hazel eyes had darkened to the same shade as his rugged, weathered tan. Her right hand rose to his cheek, still rough and unshaven, symbolic of his tough virility.

His arm encircled her, pulled her closer to him, and Darcy's body went on sensory alert. This was not fantasy, but reality, and the tremors she'd been feeling were about to culminate in a full-scale eruption. Her pulse thrummed as she tilted back her head to receive him.

His kiss was all that she'd anticipated, fulfillment of her every fantasy. His lips were firm, but yielding. His tongue tantalized, then penetrated her mouth.

Behind her closed eyelids, she saw the distant noon sun exploding and felt herself riding toward the fierce, burning halo of light. Her heart hammered like hoofbeats, and she was breathing hard when he drew away from her.

"There's something I have to tell you, Darcy."

"Yes?"

He disentangled himself from her and stood facing the fireplace. His legs were wide apart and his hands clenched behind his back, like a soldier at ease who was waiting to be disciplined. "It's the business we discussed on the ski lift."

"The priceless object?" She was confused. Business was the furthest thing from her mind. "And the crazy family?"

A sharp premonition swept through her. She knew exactly what he was going to tell her. Perhaps, she'd known all along, but had been denying it. She hadn't wanted to think he was using her. "Yes, Jonathan?"

"The family's name is Conway."

FOUR

Jonathan Hillcroft was known to be a tough competitor. Throughout the international business community, he was respected for his decisive leadership, his intellect, and his will toward unparalleled success.

As Jonathan gazed down at Darcy Conway, he felt none of those attributes. His blood ran cold, and he cursed himself for his blundering incompetence. He'd disastrously misjudged her. How the hell could she forgive him?

There was no kind rationale for his actions. No excuse. He'd brought her to Aspen to use her, to offer money in exchange for smoothing the way with her family. Of course, his strategy hadn't seemed crass when he first considered it. His proposal was logical, sensible, and he had every reason to believe she would accept it.

That was before he kissed her, and their kiss turned his clever plan upside down. He hadn't expected this inner turmoil, the desire he felt for her. He had not intended to care.

His logic had dissolved, and this lovely, black-haired, blue-eyed Irish lady had become part of his dream. He wanted her to share in his fantastic plans. "I care about you, Darcy."

She sat, still and silent. Her expression showed more than anger. Hurt? God, he hadn't meant to hurt her.

A familiar ache tightened behind his forehead. He felt his body stiffen to an armorlike rigidity, his protection.

"I don't have an excuse," he said. "I set up this trip so I could offer you a proposal."

"A bribe," she suggested.

"From what I learned about your family, I thought you'd be the most practical, the easiest . . ."

"Easiest?"

"I assumed you would be interested in a cash payout, and that you could convince the rest of them."

"You intended to use me," she said.

He could not deny it.

"Why? Jonathan, why didn't you level with me?"

"I was unsure of your reaction," he admitted. "My researchers found erratic tendencies among several members of your family, and I didn't know what to expect from you."

"Erratic tendencies?"

"Their purchase habits and bill-paying patterns are wildly irregular. As are their travel habits. Their circle of friends is ever-changing. They pursue rather unusual hobbies."

"Unusual? My mother is involved in aerobics and health food. What's so unusual about that?" Darcy bit her lower lip. She couldn't believe that she was defending Momma's "hobby," a devotion that meant her mother never walked when she could do high kicks and deep-knee bends.

In most cases, Darcy would be the first person to label her family as eccentrics. That was one of the reasons she was moving her office. However, they were *her* family, and she was offended by the idea of Jonathan and his researchers making snide inferences.

"And Poppa?" She swallowed hard. How could she make sense of her father's historical research? He re-played battles of the Civil War, occasionally mimicked Teddy Roosevelt, and in the past three Presidential elections he had voted for deceased candidates. "He's scholarly. Nothing odd about that."

"I don't mean to criticize your family. Personally, I find them very interesting."

She glared up at him. How far had he buried his tongue into his cheek to make that comment? "Really."

"Really. But I wanted to understand the lay of the land, and you seemed to be the best person to talk with."

"The least nutty?"

"Not at all."

"So, you think I'm nutty, too?"

"Of course not. I don't think any of your family is nuts."

Thank goodness, he wasn't able to read her mind. Darcy had been fantasizing about him from the moment they'd met. She carefully buried those dreams under a ton of cool hostility.

"I wanted you to come to Aspen," he said, "so I could spend some time with you, get to know you."

"You've wasted a great deal of time and effort to discover that I'm not a typical Conway. Anyone who knows me could have told you that. I'm not an eccentric dreamer."

He hesitated before answering. "I know," he said.

"And your kiss? Was that also part of your research? Have I passed your market test?"

"I apologize," he said stiffly. "I should have known better."

"From your other information? And exactly what did you find out about me?"

"You graduated from University of Chicago with a 3.6 grade point, majoring in psychology and business. You enjoy skiing. You read biographies and nonfiction. Your business is handled in a profitable, competent manner. You are discrete. Your magazine subscriptions include—"

"That's enough," she shouted.

The outrage in her voice dashed against him like a bucket of ice water. Instinctively, Jonathan felt himself rising to the challenge. A fight. He'd been in hostile negotiations all around the world. And he usually won.

But when he looked at her, his cool calculation deserted him. Her blue eyes shone hard as marble beneath her finely arched, sable eyebrows. Even angry, she was beautiful. He couldn't imagine not seeing those eyes again, discovering their sparkle when she was happy or the gleam of curiosity.

Darcy Conway represented all that he had ever wanted in a woman. Everything about her was quality. From the perfect fit of her lavender ski clothes to the healthy sheen of her curly, black hair. Her graceful posture, the way she held herself. Her gestures. Her voice. She was born a lady, he thought. Her manner, poise, and confidence could not be taught.

She rose to her feet, wincing as she moved her sprained wrist. "Please arrange for my transportation back to the lodge."

"Certainly." Yet he did not move. He couldn't. His feet had taken root on the plush carpet while his mind whirred with possibilities. He would not let her go. Not like this. "As soon as our business is concluded."

"I beg your pardon, Mr. Hillcroft. What business? I have no intention of consorting with you to betray my family."

"I paid you an advance, Ms. Conway."

"For an appraisal," she said icily. "While you

were dealing out thousand dollar bills, you neglected to mention that you expected to buy me. I'm not for sale, Mr. Hillcroft. Not at any price. I will not be used.''

"I'm not Thomas O'Bannion," he said.

"My God." She sank back on the sofa. "Your research *has* been thorough, hasn't it?"

O'Bannion had been the one piece that didn't fit in the portrait his researchers created of Darcy. In all other ways, she appeared to be utterly sensible and controlled, but her affair with O'Bannion had been foolhardy. She'd rushed after the man, allowed him to drive her car while she walked to appointments. She'd supported him and forgiven him when he forged her name on checks.

Jonathan could not comprehend why an otherwise intelligent woman would fall for a conman. But he could see the shame in Darcy's downcast eyes, and her sorrow overwhelmed his stony reserve. He sat beside her on the sofa. A fierce need rose within him. He wanted to take her in his arms, to comfort and protect her.

"Don't," she said. "Don't touch me, Jonathan."

"I see. You're still in love with O'Bannion."

"No!" Her Irish temper flared. "Mister Thomas O'Bannion is a filthy pig."

Jonathan agreed. "My market research confirms that opinion."

Her good hand clenched in a fist and she tossed her head. "It is my fervent hope that Mister Thomas

O'Bannion will rot in a gutter with the other garbage. I wouldn't give him a crust of bread if he were starving. Not a drop of water if he were dying of thirst. He's lower than dirt.''

"Scum,'' Jonathan encouraged. God, she was magnificent.

"Reptilian slime.'' Her laugh was short and bitter.

"Uglier than a wart hog.''

"Unfortunately, that's not accurate.''

"Uglier than Quasimoto?'' Jonathan urged.

"He's a fine-looking man. Quite romantic and handsome when it suits him. It's my regret that I fell for him with all the weight of my family's unreasonable eccentricity.'' Her gaze was confrontational. "I will never allow myself to lose control like that again.''

He reached to take her hand, and she snatched it away in a gesture that clearly told him to stop. "No, Jonathan, don't push me. Not yet.''

Jonathan suppressed a triumphant smile. *Not yet*, she'd said. *Not yet* implied later. He could feel the balance returning to his world. She was going to forgive him.

He rose to his feet and stretched. The tension flowed from him, and he strolled across the room and stood before the oil painting by Andrew Wyeth—a windswept seascape with pale umber and sienna tones as rich as the earth. The New England atmosphere depicted in the painting was alien to Jonathan.

Northern Californians lived a continent away from those rock-solid, Yankee values.

Gesturing to the Wyeth, he asked, ''Have you ever been to a place like this?''

''Monhegan Island off the coast of Maine.''

''What's it like?''

''Very rugged, constantly buffeted by the cold Atlantic. You'd like it, Jonathan.''

''Because I'm cold?''

She nodded. ''And hard. Your plan to bring me here, seduce me with the pleasures of skiing and use me to work on my family was extremely cold. It is, however, to your credit that you could not go through with it.''

''A warming trend?''

''We shall see.''

She was compelled to study him, to review the fine lines and tanned features. And his smile—that open, fresh, fantastic smile. What was he rally after? Was he sincere in his apology? Her anger had not yet completely dissipated, but she could feel it fading with each thump of her heart.

''I might as well know what it is,'' she said. ''What is this priceless, unique Conway possession that you wish so badly to acquire?''

''Do you feel well enough to climb a couple flights of stairs?''

''Certainly. I'm not an invalid.''

He saw the tightening of her jaw as she carefully fitted her arm into the sling. Though her complaints were good-natured about the inconvenience of splints and slings and sprains in general, he felt guilty about accidentally causing her pain. Of all the people in the world, he didn't want to hurt her. Not today, not ever.

She padded toward him in soft wool socks. Her heavy Lange ski boots had been discarded beside the door, and she seemed sweetly vulnerable without shoes. Though he was generally not a clumsy man, he reminded himself to be careful not to step on her toes with his thick-soled kletter boots. "The items I wanted you to appraise are upstairs. I think that you, of all people, will understand my obsession with these, um, properties."

She followed him to the circular brass staircase. As she ascended, she clung to the shiny pole in the center with her good right hand.

The second floor was a large, open bedroom with a king-size unmade bed. There was a phone and a small computer, but the overwhelming impression was books. Two walls were lined with books, there were books lying open on the pillow, books on the bedside table.

"Must be like sleeping in a library," she said.

"I didn't read much when I was young. Dropped out of school in seventh grade. I guess I'm trying to compensate."

She cocked her head to one side and regarded him carefully before framing her reaction. Was this his big secret? Books? "Is this what you wanted to show me?"

"Actually, I'm not all that proud of the fact that I'm too lazy to make my bed. I was in a hurry this morning to meet you." He pulled on a dangling rope causing an aluminum staircase to descend. "What I wanted to show you is up here."

She proceeded thoughtfully. This seemed like a guided tour of his personality. The first level maintained the sleek impression of a handsome, athletic bachelor who happened to have excellent taste in art.

When she looked beyond the messy kitchen and the unmade bed, she found a deeper man, one who read voraciously. From the few titles she could discern, there was an indiscriminate order to his reading—art and science, poetry and fiction.

What could possibly be lurking at the top of the aluminum staircase? He'd refered to it as an obsession.

"I'll go up first," he said, "and turn on the lights. When I had the attic remodeled, I never did find a good place for the switch. Watch your step."

She climbed after him. Her head poked level with the floor of the attic—hard wood, highly polished. Unlike the rest of the condominium, it was impeccable. No dust bunnies.

She mounted another step, then another. Sunshine poured through an overhead skylight, illuminating an old-fashioned parlor setting. Emerald green velvet loveseats faced each other in a tight symmetrical arrangement that was oddly familiar. Accents were provided by two claw-footed tables, Tiffanystyle lamps, and an ornate Oriental rug. Brass urns holding broad leafy green ferns were affixed to one wainscoated wall, and a vintage spitoon gleamed on the floor.

Darcy could see at a glance that the furnishings were not reproductions, but well-tended antiques. As she stepped into the center of the arrangement, she understood her sense of déjà vu. "This parlor setting is similar to railroad cars during the late 1800s."

"An exact replica," she heard his voice echo through the semidarkness.

Overhead lights went on, bathing the room in carefully placed, directional glow, creating the subtle effect of sunshine through side windows. Just like a railroad train. Darcy could almost feel the vibrating motion of an old-fashioned, steam locomotive as it rumbled along the tracks.

She was impressed. In all her experience, she had never seen a display of antiques that was more effective in evoking the mood of the period. Jonathan's attic reminded her of riding the night train through a genteel past.

Still, she was not prepared when she heard the whistle blow. She spun around at the low, mournful sound. "Did I imagine that?"

"Its mechanical," he explained. "Part of the 1935 Lionel model train set. I also have recordings of trains in motion. The clickety-clack of the railroad track."

She walked slowly toward him, her eyes widening with every step. The plush parlor had given her a sense of reminiscence, but it was only an entryway. The parlor was a room; the far end of the attic a kingdom. She stared in awe at the most elaborate electric train setup she had ever seen.

Jonathan flicked a switch, and a model of the Twentieth Century Limited chugged away from a domed replica of Grand Central Depot in New York at the turn of the century. A row of horse and buggies lined the street opposite the terminal, and a bright orange and blue trolley waited at a street corner. Her attention was riveted to the eight car model train as it rattled away from the station. Steam escaped through the smokestack as it traveled through the mountain passes and followed an incredibly realistic stream.

"I've taken some liberties with the route," Jonathan said. "The city of New York was, of course, more than Grand Central Depot. And I don't have Chicago depicted at all."

He stopped the train at the far end of the tracks. "This little town represents Harbor Creek, Pennsylvania, where the Twentieth Century ended its reign in 1967."

The gun metal grey engine with its bright red trim and cow catcher lurched forward on silver wheels, defying the reality of its demise.

"It's the basic O scale model, 1931," he informed her. "One of the Lionel model trains that engineer

Bob Butterfield advertised. In my complete setup, back home in California, I use the same Hudson engine, but my pullman cars are far more detailed.''

Darcy looked from the train to the man. His gaze remained on the table, unreadable. He hadn't been teasing about an obsession, she thought. It must have taken hours to construct this model. "Did you do all this yourself?"

"Yes, but I'm not a fanatic model collector. It's this particular train that fascinates me. My great-grandfather was a conductor on the Twentieth Century, and my father might have worked briefly on the New York Central line as a switchman."

"Might have?"

"I don't remember the man. He left when I was quite young."

"I'm sorry. I didn't mean to pry."

"It's not important." He reached down to make a minor adjustment on a model of a leafy oak tree. "My family connection isn't the only reason the Twentieth Century Limited intrigues me. Possibly, it's because this powerful engine heralded the new century, an era when men have walked on the moon."

"I understand why you're a Lucky Jim Conway fan," she said. "He bought several of the old cars from the Twentieth Century."

"Yes. And your family still owns them."

Darcy's eyebrows raised. He wanted to buy old railroad cars? This was getting curiouser and curiouser.

The model train completed its circuit back to the depot, and Jonathan operated the switching mechanism to send it back on its route, circling endlessly through its miniature land. His hands lifted from the controls, and he returned her gaze.

"At the risk of sounding corny, it was a proud time for our country. Nineteen-oh-two. The courageous beginnings of modern manufacturing technology." He smiled at Darcy. "So, madame appraiser, what do you think this is worth?"

"I have no idea."

"Is it enough to convince you to make me an appointment with your father and your great-aunt Louisa?"

"It's enough to convince me that you have a serious, and rather nutty obsession with this train. Tell me exactly why you want to meet with my family."

"The Twentieth Century Limited, of course. The Hudson locomotive steam engine, Number 5252, and several of the cars are owned jointly by your father and Louisa Conway Reston. You, Darcy, are the third family member I need to convince. My research shows that your father doesn't make a business move without your approval."

"Why do you want to buy a rusted out worthless train?"

"I want to refurbish the Twentieth Century, to make it fully operational for daily express runs between New York and Chicago. I've already done most of the paperwork and negotiated with Amtrak."

"But that's outrageous," she sputtered. "A train like that would surely lose money. Nobody takes trains anymore."

"I would," he said.

"It sounds like the sort of thing that someone in my family would come up with." Exactly the sort of idea she would roundly discourage, pointing out the multitude of logical reasons why it would never work. She didn't understand. Jonathan Hillcroft was supposed to be a financial genius. What on earth was he thinking of? "Perhaps there's something you haven't explained."

"I think you have the picture. I want to buy the old engine and let it run."

"And you brought me to Aspen and went through all these machinations for an out-moded, beat-up old train?"

"That's about the size of it."

"Your strategy was unnecessary," she said with an ironic laugh. "For pity sake, I have no attachment to that hunk of metal. It's just taking up space in an old barn off a railroad siding, and we would be delighted to get rid of it."

"Are you sure? It's a link with Lucky Jim."

"You don't seem to understand, Jonathan. The rest of the Conways are incurable romantics. I'm a straightforward, profit-oriented woman, concerned only with the bottom line."

"Good. Well, I'm willing to pay your asking price."

She shook her head. Here was one of the wealthiest men in the world and he was delighted as a small boy at Christmas. With such a sentimental, senseless transaction. "Why is it that when people have money they begin acting like irresponsible children?"

"It's a dream," he said.

"Oh yes, I know all about throwing away money on impossible quests. As I mentioned, my father is a scholarly man, but he's never tried to publish any of his research. My mother knows enough about nutrition to open a health food store, but when I suggested it, she just turned up her aerobics tape and did a few high kicks. Auntie Lou probably hasn't read a newspaper in years. None of them have a clue to reality."

"But everybody has dreams, Darcy."

"Take it from one who knows," she said briskly. "Life is more than shiny engines and velvet parlors."

"You're right," he said. Reaching under the table, he turned off the electricity, leaving the Twentieth Century stranded outside the tiny town that represented Harbor Creek. "Most of life is nothing more than a mundane struggle for survival. I've been luckier than most people, been in the right place at the right time with the right product. I have the ability to fulfill my dreams."

"If you want to throw your money away, I'm willing to receive it."

"You aren't at all eccentric, are you?"

"Not in the least," she confirmed.

"It's too bad. For a moment there, I had the fantasy that you might want to share my dream."

She did want to share with him, but not in a crazy, impractical fantasy. "I see this differently than you do, Jonathan. I can't idealize the railroads; their demise has cost my family a small fortune. And it's hard to get excited about Lucky Jim Conway when you know he wasn't a kindly old leprechaun. He was hard, and he was tough, a vicious competitor with a wild temper."

"A lot like you?"

"Please don't start in with comparisons," she said. "To be quite frank, you'd fit in better with the Conways than I do. Resurrecting the Twentieth Century Limited is the sort of thing they adore."

When he came around the table and gazed down upon her, Darcy recognized a harsh, cold formality. Though she'd been attacking the dreamer, she was not pleased to be face-to-face with Jonathan Hillcroft, the hard-driven businessman.

"How much?" he demanded.

She reached out to him, wanting to communicate but not finding the right words. His arm felt rigid beneath her touch, hard and unyielding as a steel train track. If flesh could feel cold, he was a man of ice.

"Name your price, Darcy."

He laid his hand on top of hers, confirming their physical contact. But that was all. His touch was chilly. She and Jonathan were very much alike. An

Ice Princess and a Man of Steel. They were two winter people who needed thick insulation to protect themselves. "I'm sorry, Jonathan. Perhaps I do want to share with you—but not on a whimsical fantasy."

"Perhaps," he said, "it would be best if we stayed with direct negotiations. I'm a very rich man, and I want the Twentieth Century. How much?"

"The price of an explanation. The simple truth. I need to know why a man who has the cleverness and will to conquer high finance is obsessed with an impossible dream."

"Nothing is impossible." He paced away from her, uncomfortable that she saw him as a Don Quixote figure, tilting at windmills. Quixote had failed, of course, and that was not Jonathan's intention. He would resurrect that train. No matter how strange or obsessive the world thought him, he would fulfill his dream.

"Please tell me, Jonathan. And I will try to understand."

"You're asking me to tell you about myself?"

"That's my price. I can't speak for Poppa or Auntie Lou, but I must have this explanation."

He sighed. Revealing himself? His carefully hidden background, his fears?

"Please, Jonathan."

"All right," he said. "I'll try to be brief. This train has come to symbolize something special to me, something I missed when I was growing up. I never spent much time being a kid. Instead, I worked. My first job was when I was six. Selling oranges on a street corner near the railroad station. I never played football or baseball. Or had friends. I hated school. My happiest time was late at night, alone in my bed before I fell asleep.

"We lived near a railroad crossing—a whistle stop—and while I awaited my dreams, there were always trains, crying and rumbling in the night. They seemed to cut through the dark with the promise to take me far away to a magical, peaceful place."

"Where is this place?"

"It's mythical. As private as a castle with a moat. Or a trip back in time to 1902. There would be no telephones. No conferences. No business meetings. A mythical place very distant from my roots."

"An escape?" she suggested.

"Perhaps."

"But it's impossible to run away. In all the world, there isn't a locomotive engine fast enough to escape from your past, from who you are."

"Isn't that why you moved your offices?"

"My move was practical," she explained. "I can run my business more efficiently, utilize my time more effectively, generate more profitability."

"What are you running away from, Darcy?"

"Precisely the sort of thing you're proposing here. Obsessions are not sensible."

He shrugged. "I guess this sounds idealistic and wildly romanticized to you. And I'll grant the facts that it's kind of silly for a grown man to play with model trains. But, damn it, this makes me happy.''

''I don't understand.''

''Yes, I can see that you don't.'' His lips drew into a smile, an insincere expression used for social occasions. ''Shall we go downstairs to conclude our discussion?''

She watched as he went toward the staircase. His shoulders were rigid; his stride was stiff. If they left the attic without resolving their differences, she knew that her relationship with Jonathan Hillcroft would be limited to superficial gains and small talk. She wanted more. Here and now, there must be a resolution.

She walked to the engineer's side of the tracks and pressed the button. A loud whistle echoed through the room, followed by a second long blast.

''If I remember my official whistle signals, that means release brakes and proceed,'' she said, flicking the switch to start the Twentieth Century on its route.

There was a short toot.

''That means stop,'' she said. ''Stop, Jonathan. I don't want you to leave.''

Slowly, he returned, his steps in rhythm with the cassette recording of a steam locomotive gathering speed. ''Yes?''

''Where are all the people?'' She gestured to the train layout spread across the table. ''There's no switchman, no engineer, no passengers. There aren't even people in the hansom cabs at the station.''

"Behind you. On the bottom shelf," he said. "I haven't gotten around to unpacking them."

"I'm glad," she said. "Because I wouldn't be any help in building bridges or trimming forests, but I can usually handle people.''

As quickly as she could with one hand, she sorted through small boxes until she found one that was full of tiny metal figures, each in its own plastic envelope. She selected a woman wearing a long, black skirt and a man in a suit and derby. "A handsome couple, don't you think?''

She winked at the little lady who stood barely two inches tall, and confided to Jonathan. "I think she's a suffragette.''

"That's good," he said, picking up the figure of the Turn of the Century man. "He wouldn't want a woman who was afraid to stand up for herself.''

Together, they placed the tiny people on the platform of Grand Central Depot to wait for their ride on the Twentieth Century Limited.

FIVE

The next day, in the early afternoon, Darcy and Jonathan stood outside a dingy barn-size building at a railroad siding in the west Chicago suburbs. They, too, made a fairly handsome couple, she thought, though not as compatible as their silent 1900s' figurine counterparts.

"The 1900s," she informed him, "were not that wonderful a period. There was child labor, rampant disease, and women were treated like chattel."

"But it was a very profitable time." He took her arm and led her away from his limousine toward the barn. "There were fortunes to be made by gutsy entrepreneurs. I should think that would appeal to you."

"Gutsy *male* entrepreneurs," she said, coming to a halt.

"I won't argue the point." He fidgeted. "Darcy, are you going to open this barn or do I have to break down the door?"

She made tracks through the dirty snow until she came to a side door where she one-handedly fitted a key into the Yale lock, turned the handle, and stepped aside. "You go first, Jonathan. It's your dream. Not mine."

He didn't argue that point, either. With quick strides, he entered the weather-beaten barn and flicked a switch beside the door. High overhead, six naked bulbs cast their dim light on Engine Number 5252 from the late Twentieth Century Limited.

The riveted steel locomotive loomed impressively huge. The main spoked wheels were nearly as tall as Darcy herself. Some of the piston arms were gnarled and broken, but the massive piece of sooty black machinery still seemed capable of powerful thrust—monstrous, steam-chugging movement.

Jonathan stood for one awestruck moment before giving a loud whoop of joy. He raced toward the beast and pulled himself up the metal stairsteps into the engineer's cab.

"Don't," Darcy shouted after him. "That thing is filthy. You're going to ruin your coat."

He appeared in the engineer's window, waved and flashed a wild-eyed, maniacal grin. "Woo-oo-oo. Damn, it's in better shape than I thought it would be."

"Would you please come down from there?"

"No way. I've dreamed about this train for a million years and I love it."

Her tongue clucked disapprovingly against the roof of her mouth, but she couldn't help smiling at his excitement as he bounded over and around the huge locomotive as if it were a jungle gym. Jonathan Hillcroft was one of the richest, most respected businessmen in the world, and he was behaving like a happy lunatic.

She strolled quietly around the barn. There were two other, less exotic railroad cars housed there and Darcy casually studied them. Bizarre seemed to be the keynote to the development of this strange relationship with Jonathan.

Last night, she'd slept at his Aspen home in a lavish guest bedroom off the living room area. As expected, Paula had returned only long enough to bring Darcy's suitcase and to introduce her latest knight in shining armor.

After an ordered-out pizza dinner, Darcy had stretched out alone on the firm mattress of the double bed. And that was when things started to become bizarre. Though Darcy had no intention of sleeping with a man she'd only known a few hours, a man who had already attempted to deceive her, every cell in her body urged her toward Jonathan's bed.

She'd tossed and turned. Though her sprained wrist hurt, the deeper ache came when she heard him moving through the house. Her sensual awareness operated like antennae. She heard the clunk of his

kletter boot on the tiled kitchen floor, then the rush
of water from the sink. Her mind pictured his throat
as he drank a glass of water. A moment later, there
was a muffled buzz from the telephone and the
answering rumble of his voice. She imagined his lips
near the telephone receiver. Then, silence. Was he
stoking the fire? Or reclining on the sofa, gazing
thoughtfully into the flames? Was he thinking of her?

She had tensed when she heard the rattle of the
circular brass staircase. He must be climbing the stair
to his bedroom. It took every ounce of her will power
to stay in her own bed.

Very, very bizarre. Darcy was amazed by her wan-
ton desire to hurl herself into his arms. She hadn't
expected to feel these reckless emotions again, and
cautioned herself to stop before she got hurt. On
some subconscious level, her warning must have
penetrated because when she finally succumbed to
sleep, she did not dream.

The next morning while they ate over-cooked
scrambled eggs and burned bacon, she'd proposed
the return trip to Chicago. Since she couldn't ski,
there was no logical reason to stay in Aspen. They
might as well begin negotiations with her family.

Purposely, she avoided mention of the more devastating reason to leave Aspen—she didn't trust herself
to keep a safe distance from Jonathan when they
were alone.

She'd held her emotions at bay during their trip

on his private jet by lecturing him on the way to win Auntie Lou and her father to his cause:

Be patient!

Never ask for something directly if there is an oblique way to reach the same conclusion.

Eat everything that is set before you.

Don't be aggressive.

Agree with everything.

Since Jonathan had the disadvantage of not being related to anyone who was listed in *Who's Who*, she advised him to use his vast assortment of rich and powerful associates to make reference points for Auntie Lou.

The idea to visit the Hudson locomotive had been his. As she shivered in the old barnlike structure, she began to regret humoring him. "Jonathan," she called out. "We really ought to be going. Where are you?"

He popped up beside her, still beaming. His trench-coat was covered with greasy filth, and when he approached her with arms outstretched, she rapidly warned him away. "Don't you dare get near me! You look like you crawled out from under a coal pile."

Still, he came closer. "Kiss me, Darcy."

"Not a chance."

"Once lightly on the lips," he demanded. "Otherwise, I'm going to grab you and smear your entire body with soot."

She reluctantly agreed. "But don't touch me."

She stood and waited until he took a position about six inches from her. Leaning slowly and carefully toward each other, their lips met chastely, a delicate taste that still managed to send electricity through her body. Bizarre, she thought. Truly bizarre.

Full of energy, he strode away from her. "This is the most wonderful day of my life."

"Aren't you forgetting something? We still need to talk with my family."

"They won't say no. They can't. This train and I were meant to be together."

"How lovely for the both of you," she drawled. "Now, shall we proceed back into the real world?"

After discarding his trenchcoat as terminally soiled and stopping at a gas station so the billionaire could wash his face, they were driven by limousine to the three-story white house where Darcy formerly kept her offices.

When Jonathan instructed the chauffeur to wait, she contradicted him. "You may return to the hotel, and Mr. Hillcroft will telephone if he needs you."

"I don't think that's wise," Jonathan said.

"Nonsense. We've decided to take the bull by the horns, confronting my father and Auntie Lou. I fully expect this to be unpleasant, Jonathan, and I don't think you should have an easy escape available."

He slapped the side of the limousine. "You heard the lady." As the long vehicle departed, Jonathan said, "You know, Darcy, I *have* been in business negotiations before."

"But those discussions were with rational people."

"Not always. Putting on a suit and sitting at a conference table doesn't guarantee a high degree of sanity."

"I assume, however, that your proposals were grounded in a presentation of logical profit-oriented facts. Not an offer on a rusted out locomotive."

He nodded. "Very true. I bow to your superior knowledge of irrational dealings with Conways."

She looked him over. Without the ruined trenchcoat, his sports jacket, casual cotton shirt, and slacks were presentable. There was, however, a hint of wild excitement in his eyes.

"You'll fit in just fine," she said, sardonically. "But remember to be patient. Auntie Lou can talk for hours without saying anything. And my father barks a lot. Before he bites."

He rolled his eyes. "This sounds like the fraternity hazing ceremonies I've read about."

"In a sense, it is," she said, leading the way up the front steps to the veranda. "You're being initiated into the Conway family confidence, and it's a very strange club."

Her brow wrinkled with worry. Unfortunately, she could not reassure him, couldn't tell him that everything would be all right. Darcy never knew what to expect from her family.

She pushed open the front door to the Conway home and ushered Jonathan into the parquet foyer. "Auntie Lou! Are you home?" To Jonathan, she whispered, "I know she's home. Saturday is cleaning day, and she doesn't trust the cleaning service to polish the silver properly."

Auntie Lou bustled down the hallway. "Darcy! Paula's mother called and told us that you've gone and hurt yourself."

"I'm really fine, Auntie Lou. It's only a sprain."

"Well I'm glad you had the good sense to come home. I'll arrange for a doctor to come while you have a nap." She belatedly greeted Jonathan. "So nice to see you again, Mr. Hale."

"Hillcroft," Jonathan corrected.

"But I'm sure you're Gertrude Hale's nephew. From Boston?"

"From California," he said.

"Oh."

Darcy winced. Her Auntie Lou considered anyone from the West Coast to be one step away from the horrors of hedonism. Anyone except the Hearsts, of course, and she wasn't *too* sure about them.

"Why don't we step into the parlor?" Darcy said.

After Auntie Lou settled in her favorite, antimacassar-draped chair, she fixed Jonathan with a stern gaze. "I've always said there was too much sunshine in California, don't you agree?"

"Absolutely." He nodded. "Unhealthy. Bad for the skin."

She studied him carefully. "You seem to have a bit of a tan, Mr . . . what was it again?"

"Hillcroft."

"Hillcroft. I shall try to remember, but it's such an unusual name."

"Yes, indeed," Darcy said. "Isn't that exactly what your good friend, Wallace Kerby-Barnett, told you, Jonathan?"

"You know the Kerbys?" Auntie Lou asked brightly.

"Wonderful family," Jonathan replied with a nod.

"Except for the youngest daughter." Her eyes widened and she leaned forward. "You know the one I mean? That cute little redhead. It's simply scandalous, the way she's taken up with that film actor."

While her great-aunt Louisa happily dissected the foibles and flaws of the Kerby family, Darcy watched Jonathan sink into a polite stupor. He nodded and murmured his agreement with each and every one of Auntie Lou's statements. Very good, she thought. Now, it was time to add her father to the social mix.

"You two seem to be getting along," she said. "I'll fetch some tea, shall I?"

"Whatever you'd like," Auntie Lou said. "It's so lovely to chat with someone like dear Jonathan, someone who has a sense of history. Are you sure you're not related to the Boston Hales?"

"I'm sure."

"It's just as well, I suppose. The family has such poor health, you know . . ."

Darcy fled down the hall. The situation was ironic. She'd left her family home for the express purpose

of escaping their peculiarities, and now she was trying to introduce Jonathan into their bosom. Bizarre,
indeed.

She whipped through the kitchen, rustled up a
respectable tea and cookies arrangement on a rolling
tea cart, and wheeled down the hall. Taking a deep
breath, she rapped three times on the door to her
father's study and entered the walnut panelled room.
As usual, it was filled with dusty tomes and cigar
smoke. "Hi, Poppa."

"Aren't you in Colorado?"

"Sprained my wrist," she said. "I couldn't ski,
so I decided to come back here."

"To live here?" he questioned hopefully.

Her father, Adam Conway, had made it clear that
he disapproved of Darcy leaving home. She was the
youngest of four children, unmarried, and it was his
frequently stated belief that it was his duty to take
care of her. Never mind that his idea of caretaking
meant time-consuming forays to museums and librarys
to study objects in which Darcy had no interest. Or
lectures on Teddy Roosevelt and the Rough Riders.

"I'm only here for a visit," she said, firmly.

"Too bad." He pushed his gold frame glasses up
on his nose to study the splint on her arm. "You
ought to be more careful, Darcy. If you go bashing
around in the world all by yourself with no one to
take care of you, there are going to be some hurts.
That arm is graphic evidence, my girl. Now, I know
you like to think you're independent and all—"

"I am independent."

"—but you don't have to be. You've got family, Darcy. You must never forget where you came from."

Darcy wondered how Jonathan would react to that advice. In their conversations, she had seldom seen anyone so determined to bury his past.

"Back in Lucky Jim's day," her father muttered, "women were ladies, didn't go off and sprain their arms."

"I brought someone home with me, Poppa. His name is Jonathan Hillcroft, and I think you'll enjoy meeting him. You have a lot in common."

Her father rocked back on his heels. "You're up to something, my girl. What's the real reason you want me to meet this Hillcroft fellow?"

"I'll let you talk with him and find out." She took her father's arm and led him into the hall. "He happens to be a great fan of Lucky Jim."

"He isn't like that O'Bannion character, is he?"

"Not in the least," Darcy assured him. She noticed a possessive gleam in her father's eye, a gleam that usually meant trouble. "Maybe it's better if you don't meet Jonathan."

"Nonsense, it's important for a father to take an interest in his daughter's social life. But I shall keep in mind the immortal words of President Teddy Roosevelt: Speak softly and carry a big stick."

Darcy groaned inwardly. Her father had not spoken softly in his life. "Poppa, this is in the line of a business proposal."

"Hillcroft thinks he's a businessman, does he? We'll see."

Her father surged ahead of her and burst into the parlor, immediately engaging Jonathan in an overly-vigorous handshake.

While Auntie Lou served the tea along with a liberal dose of chatter, Darcy watched Adam and Jonathan studying each other warily. Apparently, this was her father's idea of speaking softly, and it didn't last long.

He lit a cigar and said, "Well, Hillcroft, my daughter tells me you're interested in Lucky Jim."

"I'm a great admirer of his."

"What do you suppose old Jim would say about this fancy cookies and tea snack?"

"He'd reach for the Irish whiskey."

Adam barked a smug, superior laugh. "That's a typical mistake, Hillcroft, assuming that my grandfather, a hard-headed Irishman, was a heavy drinker. But, of course, you're dead wrong. To be sure, Lucky Jim took a drop now and again, but he was careful."

Jonathan nodded. "You're the expert."

Darcy nodded. Very good. Jonathan hadn't risen to the bait by engaging in an unwinnable argument with Poppa.

"What business are you in, Hillcroft?"

"I started in real estate."

"How nice," Auntie Lou put in. "I've always said that land is the best investment. And so did my legendary grandfather, Lucky Jim. By the way, Adam, you're mistaken about his drinking habits. I remember clearly that grandpa loved his whiskey."

"Stow it, Louisa," Adam said, not unpleasantly. "I want to hear more about what Hillcroft does for a living. I've got an idea that I've heard something about him."

"You have not," Auntie Lou snapped. "He's not one of the Boston Hales."

"But I do know him. Unless I miss my guess, he's one of those corporate pirates, isn't he?"

"Corporate raider," Darcy corrected.

"Whatever. Hillcroft goes in and buys up businesses, puts everybody out of work, then sells it for a tax write-off."

"That's not exactly accurate," Jonathan said.

Darcy noticed a degree of change in Jonathan. A coolness. The friendly smile faded from his eyes, and she tried to call off her father's determined affront. "Jonathan's corporations employ thousands of people all around the world."

"Worldwide, eh?"

Her father took a puff on his cigar, and Darcy cringed, knowing that the "big stick" was about to land its first blow.

"Well, Hillcroft. I sure hope you're not one of those fellows who doesn't think the U.S.A. is good enough."

"No, sir, if it weren't for good old capitalism, I would not exist."

"Oh my," Auntie Lou fluttered. "How like grandfather!"

"And that's what worries me," Adam muttered. "Tell me, Hillcroft, what exactly does a corporate raider do?"

"In very basic terms, I take over mismanaged businesses and straighten them out. For a profit."

"I knew it. That's taking advantage." Apparently, her father thought he'd made a point because he leaned close to Darcy and confided, "Not exactly fair play, is it? Coming in and reaping the rewards of a small businessman's sweat."

"You don't understand." Darcy wanted to halt him, but she knew it was as futile as trying to stop a runaway train. He was in high gear, his eyes twinkling behind his glasses.

"Did you know, Hillcroft, that my daughter is in business for herself? Are you planning on raiding her? I'll tell you, my boy, you might as well be a pirate with a Jolly Roger flag hung over the front of your limousine."

"I don't plunder. The employees of a business under my control don't suffer. Their jobs are secure, more secure once the company they work for is operating efficiently."

"You mean to tell me that you've never laid off?"

"Never. That is one of my requirements for takeover."

"How come?" Adam wasn't in the least bothered by his illogical flip-flop. "Doesn't sound like good business sense."

"Because, Mr. Conway, I know what it means to be unemployed." Jonathan gazed coldly over the rim of the china teacup. "Do you?"

"I sure as heck do, sonny." Adam returned the glare. "I've been unemployed most of my life."

Darcy winced. Of course her father had been unemployed. He'd never had to work! This conversation had gone from hostile to ludicrous, and that did not bode well for Jonathan's negotiations. It would take a combination Emily Post and Dr. Joyce Brothers to soothe these troubled waters.

She didn't think things could get worse until she heard her father say, "Do you know what Lucky Jim's real passion was?"

"No!" Darcy exclaimed. "You're not going to do this."

"I know," Auntie Lou bubbled. "Grandpa Jim loved pugilistic displays. Like Jack Dempsey, you know."

"What do you say, Hillcroft?" Adam Conway peeled off his glasses and clambored to his feet. His bobbing and weaving were fairly agile for a sixty-year-old man. "There's a ring in the basement. How about if you and I duke it out a few rounds?"

"No, sir, I don't think so."

"What's the matter, sonny? Afraid of an old man?"

"He doesn't want to hurt you," Darcy growled. "Now sit down and quit behaving like this."

"Doesn't want to hurt me?" Adam punched at Jonathan's arm. "Hah! I was middle-weight champ on the Yale boxing team."

"Stop it!" Darcy shouted.

When her father's hand flicked again, slapping Jonathan's cheek, he provoked a reaction. Jonathan came to his feet in a single, fluid move. His body tensed. Instinctively, his hands drew into loose fists and his weight centered on the balls of his feet. Though he had never been on a boxing team, he knew how to fight. When he was growing up, he'd learned on the street, the hard way.

He forced himself to relax, seeking the detachment that served him so well in business negotiations. Nothing would be gained from sparring with Darcy's father. He trained his lips into a smile. "I will have to decline your invitation to spar, Mr. Conway. I certainly don't want to climb into the ring with one of Yale's finest."

"A big, strong guy like you? You're not a sissy, are you? I don't want my daughter hanging around with any sissies." He chuckled and jabbed again at Jonathan's arm. "Come on, boy. I've missed this. I used to go in the ring with my sons. And I'd beat them, too."

"I'll bet you did." Jonathan lowered himself into the chair. He could see that the old man was already panting from the exertion and feared that Darcy's father was working himself into some kind of collapse. Hoping to defuse the situation, he asked, "Were you a Jack Dempsey fan?"

"Yes, indeed." He slapped at Jonathan's elbow. "Dempsey.

"Floyd Patterson." He jabbed again.

"Rocky Marciano." Another slap.

With lightning reflex, Jonathan caught the old man's fist and held it. His words came through clenched teeth. "I won't fight with you, Adam."

"Both of you," Darcy snapped. "Stop this right now. You're being ridiculous."

"Not me," her father said, shaking free of Adam's grasp. "I'm not the sissy who's sitting there eating cookies and drinking tea."

It was at that moment that Darcy's mother bounded gracefully into the room. She was wearing a form-fitting yellow and blue striped leotard. "Darcy, my sweet. I didn't know you were here, but I'm so glad. Paula's mother said you'd been hurt. Let me see your arm, dear. You might need an aloe soaked poultice."

"Not now, Momma," Darcy said. "This is Jonathan Hillcroft."

"I'm Emma Conway." She shook Jonathan's hand. "Please excuse my outfit, but I had an aerobics class this afternoon."

"Get dressed, Emma," her husband snapped.

"Just as soon as I'm ready, Adam." She turned to her daughter. "By the way, Darcy, there was a rather urgent telephone message from your new secretary. What's her name? Oh yes, Karen. She said half of your files had been lost.''

"Oh my God." Darcy glanced from the two angry men to giggling Auntie Lou to Emma. Her mother seemed the sanest of the bunch. "Momma, I have to call my secretary. Don't let them do anything until I get back. Is that clear?''

"Perfectly. Now, tell me, Mr. Hillcroft, what do you do for a living?''

"He's a pirate," Adam crowed.

"I doubt that, dear. All the pirates were laid to rest when your grandfather's casket sank into the earth.''

Darcy groaned, but raced to the library across the hall and rang her office. Surely her father and Jonathan could manage not to kill each other for a few minutes.

The telephone rang. And rang. It was Saturday afternoon, of course. Her secretary wouldn't be there. After three calls to information, she found Karen Parelli's home phone and punched out the numbers on the touch tone.

She had just reached her secretary when she saw the procession heading toward the boxing ring in the basement. Her mother waved as she passed the library door. "Don't worry, Darcy. It's just a workout. They've promised not to hurt each other.''

"Sure," she muttered. "They're going to put on leather gloves and punch each other in the face. But it won't hurt.''

"What?" Her new secretary's voice came through

the telephone receiver. "Ms. Conway, I'm on my way out the door. Can this wait until Monday?"

"The files," Darcy demanded. "What happened to the files?"

Her secretary's explanation of a mix-up with the moving van took five minutes and did not reassure Darcy. Her office building was newly available, and four tenants had chosen the same day to move in. Apparently, the boxes for Original Property Brokers had been confused with those from another office.

Darcy groaned. All of the information in her files was confidential. If it fell into the wrong hands, major embarrassments would ensue.

"I'll go there this afternoon," she told her secretary.

"Should I meet you?"

"I'll handle it."

She hung up the telephone and plunged down the stairway to the basement.

Jonathan and her father were already stripped to their shirtsleeves, stalking around the square canvas ring. Her mother and Auntie Lou shouted encouragement from the corners. This was a nightmare, Darcy thought. How had she ever expected to ease Jonathan into her family without a squabble? They were too crazy. What on earth was her father trying to do, needling and prodding like that? And why had Jonathan risen to the bait?

She was tempted to simply walk away and let them get what they deserved. Let Poppa get his silly nose broken. Let Jonathan lose his chance for negotiations. But she couldn't do that. Someone had to take care of these idiots, and unfortunately, someone's name was Darcy.

Though Jonathan was obviously holding back, doing nothing more than blocking her father's jabs, she could not allow this to continue. "Jonathan," she shouted.

He turned at the sound of her voice, and her father landed a hard left cross on his chin. Jonathan's head snapped back. But he still did not retaliate against the older man.

When Adam drew back his arm for a roundhouse right, Jonathan sidestepped the blow, and Darcy's father went spiraling across the ring, bounced off the ropes, and sat down hard on the canvas.

"Poppa!" Darcy ran to the ring. By the time she'd climbed through the ropes, her father was back on his feet.

He spat the protective mouthpiece into his glove. "That was a lucky shot, Hillcroft."

"He didn't touch you," Darcy said.

"What do you mean, my girl? I didn't go flying across this ring on my own steam. Of course, he touched me. Didn't you?"

She looked to Jonathan to deny her father's accusation. Instead, he removed his own mouthpiece and said, "I did get in a lucky punch. It was so fast, Darcy, you didn't see it."

"I'll say it was." Adam swung his heavy glove

around Darcy and punched Jonathan's arm. "Are you sure you've never sparred before?"

"Not formally." Jonathan playfully returned the old man's jab, jolting him off balance. "But I'm a fan of club fighting."

"And that's the really rough stuff. Did you hear that, Emma? I've been in the ring with a club fighter."

Darcy glared from one man to the other. "This is some kind of stupid macho game, isn't it? Well, I want it stopped. And I want it stopped now."

Auntie Lou rang the bell at the side of the ring. "That's Round One," she called out. "And I really think it ought to go to Darcy."

Emma had also climbed through the ropes. "I agree with Darcy. You boys have worked up a sweat, undoubtedly elevating your pulse rates, and enough is enough."

Jonathan and Adam shrugged and returned to their corners.

While Darcy struggled to one-handedly unlace Jonathan's gloves, she hissed, "This was so silly. I cannot believe you got in the ring with him."

"I couldn't avoid it. I was afraid he'd have a heart attack with all that bobbing and weaving in the parlor."

"Men! After I wasted so much time giving you instructions on how to endear yourself to my family. You allowed him to bait you, Jonathan. This was outrageous. Not to mention that you could have hurt him, really hurt him."

"You know I wouldn't do that."

"How could I possibly know that?" In frustration over her inability to unfasten the lacing, she held up her splinted wrist. "Look what you did to me."

She regretted the words as soon as they'd left her mouth. An odd expression passed across his features, fading to harsh resignation.

"I'm sorry," she said. "I didn't mean to say that you'd hurt me on purpose. I know it was an accident. Oh, Jonathan—"

"It's all right," he said, but he felt the burden of his tough, street-fighting background. Would a more civilized man have climbed into the ring with her father? "Perhaps you're right, Darcy. I'll never fit in with a family like the Conways. I was made differently."

"No, Jonathan. I didn't mean that."

"I was wrong to attempt to use you. And it's wrong to mislead your family." He forced the boxing gloves from his wrists, picked up his jacket, and marched across the ring. "Adam. Louisa. I have a proposition for you."

Their eyes focused upon him, and he continued. "I want to buy Engine 5252."

"Buy the Twentieth Century?" Adam Conway said, rotating his shoulder. "That's what you're here for?"

"Yes, sir, that's why I wanted to meet you."

"Why didn't you say so in the first place? We could have saved ourselves a lot of trouble, Hillcroft."

"I think it's a lovely idea," Auntie Lou said, bustling to take the men's boxing gloves.

Adam took Jonathan by the arm. "Let's go up to my office and talk turkey. You know, Hillcroft, you've got a good uppercut, but your jab could use some work."

Darcy sank down on the three-legged stool in Jonathan's corner. After her massive dose of advice and instruction, the direct approach turned out to be the most effective. The easiest. All she had really needed to do was open the door for Jonathan.

Her mother knelt beside her. "What's the problem, dear? You look distressed. You've been taking your vitamin C, haven't you?"

Darcy watched Jonathan's broad shoulders disappear up the staircase and listened to the rumble of his laughter. He was moving away from her. Now that he'd found a tentative ground for negotiating with her father and Auntie Lou, he didn't need her anymore.

Her mother fondly stroked the black curls away from her face. "Are you in pain, Darcy? Is your wrist hurting you?"

"No, Momma. It's my heart."

SIX

During the next two weeks, Jonathan buzzed in and out of Chicago with constant frequency. His other business concerns took him to faraway places, especially to his main offices in northern California, but he couldn't stay away from the train. He kept coming back, like a hummingbird to a feeder.

He arranged for the once proud Hudson Engine to be moved to suitable warehousing for repairs and renovation, and it broke his heart to see her dragged helplessly over the rails. Likewise, as her pieces were shined and refitted, he rejoiced over the transformation. She would be beautiful and strong once again.

His negotiations for the purchase of Engine Number 5252 concluded with a cooperative settlement. Adam and Louisa agreed to sell seventy percent ownership to Jonathan while retaining ten percent apiece and ten percent for Darcy.

And there was his problem, the one murky area in an otherwise bright picture. He didn't know what to do about Darcy.

Everytime he saw her or heard her voice or caught the lingering scent of her perfume in the Conway home, he knew she was the only woman for him. Yet when they were face-to-face, a strange chemistry repelled them. He would advance. She would retreat. Then he would retreat to the emotional safety of aloof silence. And she would begin to warm up to him.

Sometimes, he thought they were much too different to ever share a relationship. He liked to dream; she prefered facts. Her childhood had been pampered; his was one ragged-edged, painful disaster after another. She was a lady. He was a street kid who made good.

What to do about Darcy?

It was after nine o'clock on a Monday when Jonathan instructed his chauffeur to take him to her new apartment. He pressed the front bell and waited for her to answer.

"Jonathan? What are you doing here?"

"We had a meeting," he said. "Your father, Auntie Lou, you, and I. But you never showed."

"I had a headache. I'm sure whatever you decided was fine."

"As a ten percent owner of the Twentieth Century, you should be made aware of recent developments."

"Please come in." She pushed open the door but allowed him to close it behind himself. It was vital to her control to avoid physical contact with him. Yet when he stepped into her apartment, his presence seemed to fill the entire space, permeating her senses with an awareness she could not dissolve.

He glanced at the cozy pastel surroundings. "Very attractive. You've been busy."

"Yes."

Very, very busy. Her antidote for confusion was action. Not only had she rented and furnished the apartment, but she'd established policies for Original Property Brokers. After locating the missing files which were—thankfully!—unopened, she'd launched an advertising campaign and had trained her secretary, Karen Parelli. Three new clients had engaged her to explore loan possibilities.

There should have been a hundred reasons for her to celebrate, instead she was overwhelmed with anxieties. Her efficient career, on her own at last, seemed vacant and lonely.

"Darcy, you haven't come to see the progress on the train."

"That's right, I haven't. As you noticed, I've been busy."

"I couldn't help notice," he said. "Everytime I come to Chicago, I call you. I've invited you to dinner, to lunch, to brunch, to a play, to a performance at the Lyric Opera. Everytime, you've turned me down.''

''But we've met. At my parents' house.'' Where it was safe, she thought. Her family, by their nature, prevented privacy or intimacy. And she couldn't stand to be alone with Jonathan, like now. The thought was too heart-wrenching.

She didn't know what to expect from him and didn't trust herself to control her emotions. Always, there was the fear that when his dealings with her family were complete, he would disappear. Accidentally, he would hurt her. Again.

''What was it you wanted to tell me about the train?''

He settled on the mint green sofa. ''We considered a precise replication of the engine, maintaining the integrity of a steam locomotive.''

''Ridiculous! I'm sure there are pollution regulations about steam engines.'' She picked up her needlepoint and began working furiously. ''Besides, why would you want to recreate an out-moded technology?''

''Steam is so charming. It makes those great noises.''

''Like someone blowing their nose?''

''Like a mysterious whisper, too soft to hear the words.''

She knew that sound. It came with her memories of Aspen and their time together in the barn, beckoning her to a reckless, unknown destination.

"What about speed?" she asked, stabbing at her needlepoint. "Steam engines aren't as fast as diesel."

"We can't utilize full speed anyway. Even if we're going nonstop express there are eighteen necessary slow-downs. The best running time would be an average of seventy miles per hour. Which means the one-way trip is roughly fourteen hours."

"Roughly? That certainly doesn't sound like Vanderbilt's Twentieth Century. Their timetable was precise."

"Which is why we're going to have to schedule a test run before we open to the public. We need to check out the comfort factors and the timing."

She laid her needlepoint work in her lap. "Have you ever heard of the Hikari trains that run between Tokyo and Osaka?"

"Of course," he scoffed.

"Now that's a system I could get enthusiastic about," she said. "A state of the art railroad, fully electric, two hundred mile per hour capability, very sleek. They depart every fifteen minutes and arrive on schedule."

"They look like beached dolphins," he said. "And they miss the whole point of railroading."

"Silly me, and I thought efficient service was the purpose of a transportation system."

"That's one goal, but the main focus for the Twentieth Century is luxury travel—relaxation and a genteel atmosphere."

"I'm not impressed. The Hikari system gets my vote."

"Darcy, I came here to talk about something other than trains. We have some important issues to discuss. About us."

"Not now, Jonathan." She tried to keep the panic from her voice. "I hate to be rude, but it's late and I'm tired and—"

"When?" he demanded. "You can't put me off forever."

His determined expression warned her that further evasion was useless. The least she could hope for was to postpone the inevitable confrontation, the final dissolution when they faced the fact that a relationship was impossible between two such different people. She was a modern woman, not a dreamer. She would never relinquish her self-control. Why didn't he see that? All they would ever accomplish together would be to find new ways to hurt each other.

"I want your answer, Darcy. When?"

"Thursday," she said. "After dinner, at my parents' house."

"Fine." He rose to his feet and before she could manufacture another excuse, he was at the door. "Thursday."

At nine o'clock on Thursday, she joined her father and Jonathan in her father's office where the two men were making a great show of drinking brandy and smoking huge, thick cigars.

Darcy opened a window. "How can you see through this pollution?"

"These are Havanas," her father informed her. "A man's pleasure. What was it Rudyard Kipling said, Johnny?"

"A woman is only a woman, but a good cigar is a smoke."

"How quaint," Darcy said. "Well, I see you two are regressing nicely. Why don't I come back when you've grown up?"

"Hold on, Missy." Her father stubbed his cigar out in the ashtray. "I need to talk to you."

She perched on one of the heavy leather chairs in the office, carefully avoiding Jonathan's gaze. "Yes, Poppa?"

"We've hit a snag in our planning," he said genially. "Louisa and I think the test run for the Twentieth Century is a fine idea, but we'd like it to start off with a bang. Hoopla."

"I've offered to turn my publicity department loose on the concept," Jonathan put in.

"But that's not enough, Johnny."

Her father leaned back in his chair, and Darcy recognized an uncanny resemblance to Lucky Jim. Was it possible, after all these years, that her father would become a businessman?

"Louisa and I agree," he said. "Johnny is the major owner, and owners have got to support their businesses. That's the American way. So, if we've got a big, fancy opening scheduled, Johnny's got to be there.''

Darcy immediately recognized the problem: Jonathan's reputation and his distaste for publicity. If the reclusive Jonathan Hillcroft scheduled an appearance, there were bound to be hundreds of curiosity seekers.

"We were thinking of a charity benefit," Adam Conway said. "For the first month's operation, half the price of every ticket would go to the migrant farmers in California. So, Johnny, what do you say?"

"I'm considering it."

In surprise, Darcy gaped at him. His expression was calm and thoughtful. And handsome, she helplessly added. He'd removed his tie and unfastened the first two buttons on his silk shirt, and she could see the tantalizing hint of dark chest hair curling toward his collar.

"Darcy," her father said. "I want you to convince him."

"Me?" she squeaked.

"That's right. And, by the way, I have another matter to discuss. This time, my question is for Johnny." His eyebrows lowered and he pushed his glasses back onto his nose. "Mister Hillcroft, sir, Darcy's mother and I have been wondering. What exactly are your intentions concerning our daughter?"

"I beg your pardon?"

"This is not 1902," Darcy muttered.

Her father shushed her. "I don't expect you to

understand, little lady. This is something menfolk need to discuss. Your intentions, sir?''

''Honorable,'' Jonathan replied.

Terrific, Darcy thought. If there was anything she wanted from Jonathan, it was to be physically ravished, and these two ''menfolk'' were pretending to be characters in an eighteenth century farce. Honorable intentions? The next thing they'd be doing was discussing her dowry. ''Now that we have these significant questions out of the way, I'll leave you 'gentlemen' to your brandy.''

''Darcy,'' Jonathan called to her. ''We have an appointment. Shall we go for a walk?''

''Good man,'' her father encouraged. ''I myself popped the question to Emma while we were stepping out at Grant Park in Chicago.''

''Excuse us, Adam,'' Jonathan took Darcy's elbow and hustled her through the door before she could respond to her father's comment.

By the time he'd grabbed their coats from the hall closet and ushered her through the front door to the veranda, she was ready to explode. ''What was that all about?''

''Damned if I know.''

''Acting like some idiot gentry. Puffing on cigars. Quoting Kipling. Honorable intentions? What does that mean?''

He led her down the stairs to the sidewalk. ''It means exactly what it says. I respect you.''

''Thanks.''

He held her long grey wool coat. When she slipped her arms inside, his hands lingered on her shoulders for a fraction of a second too long. Then he donned his own camel hair overcoat.

His touch had wakened her senses and reminded her of her need to be prudent, not to be alone with him. "Jonathan? It's kind of chilly outside. Maybe we'd better stay here and talk."

He closed the door to the house. Porchlight spilled over them as he confronted her. "Two weeks ago, you told me how to deal with your family. You said to be patient. And, Darcy, I've been so patient with you that it hurts. I can't wait any longer."

Patient with her? She nodded curtly. "Let's walk."

They descended the stair and circled the driveway in silence. She fell in step beside him, and they strolled along the sidewalk. It was February, but the weather had been uncommonly warm. Though traces of snow remained at the leeward side of thick oak trees, the sidewalk was dry, and their bootheels resounded against the concrete.

The night air swirled mist around their ankles. The wind whipped a moist blush to her cheeks. Their pace was casual as they passed beneath street lamps and through the shadows of the barren, leafless trees bordering the sidewalk.

Darcy knew this area like the palm of her hand, but tonight it seemed pleasantly unfamiliar, as if she were discovering for the first time that the neighbors had a wrought iron fence, and their dog was a golden retriever.

"How's your wrist?" he asked.

She kept her hands in her pockets. "Better than the doctor said it would be. I'm only wearing an Ace bandage, and I take that off at night."

"Maybe it wasn't as serious a sprain as we thought."

"Maybe I'm a fast healer." She knew it wasn't true for emotional hurts; those took forever to mend.

"I'm gong to Aspen tomorrow," he said. "Would you come with me?"

"To ski?"

"Of course, we'll ski."

"Only to ski?" she persisted.

"All right, Darcy, I've learned my lesson. I won't attempt to be less than one hundred percent honest with you. I have an ulterior motive for inviting you to Aspen. I want to spend time alone with you."

How could anything sound so delicious and so potentially hurtful at the same time? Like eating chocolate, it tasted so wonderful that she could eat five full boxes, but she hated the pounds it could add to her hips. Cautiously, she asked, "Why, Jonathan?"

"I think you know."

"I might have suspicions, but I haven't heard a clear declaration of facts." She paused. "And don't try to brush me off with something as vague as honorable intentions."

He took a deep breath and exhaled slowly. "This

is so typical of you, Darcy. You want my intentions spelled out in detail. In triplicate? Shall I prepare a contract covering all eventualities?''

''I want to avoid misunderstandings.''

''Is that why you've been avoiding me?''

She didn't answer, and he took her silence to indicate assent. Though he couldn't deny they'd been plagued by misunderstandings, her decision to stay away from him would never lead to a resolution.

He'd been so damn frustrated for the past two weeks. Each attempt to reach her was rebuffed. Each invitation was refused. Yet he was driven to try and try again. She was becoming almost as much of an obsession as the train. ''I've missed you.''

''How could you miss me? We barely know each other.''

''Strictly speaking, that's correct. Absolutely logical, factual, sensible.''

''But it's not right.'' Her voice was a whisper. ''I've missed you, too.''

A sense of relief warmed him. This small, glimmering sliver of hope reassured him that he wasn't completely out of his mind in pursuing a woman who had rejected him at every turn. He believed the glimmer more than the solid wall of ice she'd constructed around herself. It was impossible for him to be experiencing such desire and not to have it reciprocated. Somewhere deep inside, he knew that she cared, in some small way, she cared for him. He'd heard it in her voice when she greeted him.

He'd felt it whenever they touched. Her body responded to him with appealing tremors and a warm flush that rose from her throat to her forehead. And, always, her eyes betrayed her, reflecting her excitement and shining with anticipation.

They reached the street corner and paused before stepping down the curb and crossing the street.

"This used to be my boundary," she confided. "Whenever I ran away from home, I'd never make it farther than this corner."

"A change of heart?"

"Not really. I had to go back. I wasn't allowed to cross the street by myself."

He gazed at the gracious homes surrounding them. Light glowed warmly from their windows, suggesting a coziness within. "I can't imagine running away from this."

"Even after you've met my family?"

He laughed. "They're not so bad, Darcy."

"You're right. They're very endearing people, kind and well-meaning. It's just that I'm different from them. I'm pragmatic. They're dreamers and eccentrics. For them, romantic notions are second nature."

"But not for you?"

She sighed. "Let's just say I'm more comfortable with the factual evidence."

"Ah ha! But facts can lead to romance. For example, we have agreed, both of us, that we've missed each other. Fact."

"That's interesting. Please continue."

"There is an attraction between us. A level of magnetism. Fact."

"On a purely theoretical level, I would agree with that."

"Another fact: You've been fighting this attraction."

"No more than you, Jonathan."

"That's where you're wrong. I'll admit that I'm not always a real warm guy, but I'm not fighting this. Besides, how can you say more or less?"

"I'm sure it can be measured," she said. "There must be someway to figure a relative degree on emotions or attractions."

"What does that mean, Darcy?"

"I guess it boils down to: Can you hurt me more than I could hurt you?"

"I see it another way," he said. "Can I please you more than you can please me?"

She halted beneath a street lamp and confronted him. "I doubt that."

Just like a Conway, he thought, always ready to battle the competition. "Prove it."

Darcy grinned. "You think I won't?"

"Right here on this respectable street in Maple Grove, Illinois? No, I think you're much too proper for that."

"That shows how little you know me."

"I repeat: Prove it."

She took a step toward him. Her hands came out of her pocket and caressed the soft, rich fabric of his coat. She peeked flirtatiously at him through her thick black eyelashes as her fingers fondled and unfastenend the four leather covered buttons of his coat.

"How am I doing so far?" she asked.

"Not too badly," he teased.

"Hang onto your socks, baby. Because I have not yet begun to fight."

She slid her arms inside his coat and hugged him, pressing the length of her body against him. He was so warm, so vibrant. God, it felt so good to hold him, to be close.

When his arms closed around her, she felt a warning tremble from deep within her. It would have been practical to stop, to end this game before it got out of hand. But she didn't want to. An instinctive urge overtook her common sense, and she brazenly fitted her leg between his and rubbed against him with slow sensual strokes.

Wrapped in his embrace, she reached up to stroke his clean-shaven cheek. The lamplight shone in his sandy hair and emphasized the strong angle of his jaw.

"Am I pleasing you, Jonathan?"

"Yes, you are," he confirmed, huskily. "Even more than I expected."

The tension in his voice excited her. Cradled to his chest, she felt his heartbeat accelerate to a throbbing pace.

Her hand slipped behind his neck. She tilted back

her head, went up on tiptoe and pulled his mouth toward hers.

Though she'd intended to kiss him lightly with teasing nips that would drive him wild, her hunger was too voracious. Their lips met, and her control vanished. Prudent sensibility was gone.

She was no longer coyly meeting his challenge. Her need for him was elemental, insatiable. The strength from every fiber in her body went into that kiss. The pressure was unbearable, yet utterly fulfilling.

Darcy felt herself transported from a chilly street in the Chicago suburbs to that distant place he'd described, that mythical place where haunting train whistles heralded the beginning of beautiful dreams.

A car drove past them, encouraging the lovers with a friendly honk, and Darcy broke away. The headlights startled her back to reality.

"Will you come to Aspen with me?" he asked. "Tonight?"

"Tonight," she said. It was no longer a question. She would go with him anywhere, on any journey.

SEVEN

When they took off at one o'clock in the morning from Midway Airfield, Jonathan and Darcy were not alone on his private jet. Two businessmen from a London corporation accompanied them.

In usual circumstances, Darcy would have been delighted to participate in a conversation about stocks and trends and multinational corporate operations. Tonight, however, these sharp businessmen were an unwelcome intrusion.

After one quick stop at her apartment to toss essentials into her suitcase, she'd decided to cast caution to the winds, to fulfill the desire she'd felt toward Jonathan from the first time they'd met. The last thing she wanted was to be chaperoned by a couple of gentlemen with briefcases and flow charts.

After takeoff, the four of them sat around a comfortable oak table, sipping coffee and nibbling at cheeses from the well-stocked refrigerator and bar. They chatted about the prospect of skiing at Aspen and the fates of their favorite football teams, and then a fairly detailed business discussion ensued. Before long, the table was littered with documents, printouts, and legal pads.

Darcy's gaze impatiently sought Jonathan's lips, willing him to strap these extraneous executives into parachutes and deploy them from the plane. While they talked about the impact of the new Federal tax policies, she imagined what it would be like to make love in a jet, ten thousand feet in the sky. She remembered the warmth of Jonathan's embrace, and his challenging promise to please her more than she could please him. Sweet anticipation trickled through her. How would he please her? What tender methods would he employ?

A voice penetrated her reverie. "What's your opinion, Ms. Conway?"

Darcy regarded the nice-looking blond man as though he were a being from another planet. "My opinion?"

She glanced over at Jonathan. His grey eyes were positively smouldering. "What were you thinking about, Darcy?"

He knew darn well what she was thinking about. "Excuse me, gentlemen. I've had a long day."

When she rose from her seat and moved to the dimly lit rear of the jet, Jonathan followed. They sat, side-by-side, on a highbacked reclining sofa facing away from the other men. Though they were only six feet from the table, the steady purr of the engine insulated their conversation.

"No bed," Jonathan said. "Bad planning on my part."

"What are you talking about?"

"I prefer to take this smaller jet in and out of Aspen, but it doesn't have a separate compartment. No bed."

"There would be enough room, if you hadn't insisted upon bringing along Tweedledee and Tweedledum." She chuckled. "They're both so deadly serious and businesslike. Maybe I should call them Mr. Scrooge and Mr. Cratchit."

"Another instance of my bad planning," he confirmed. "But if these matters are settled tonight, we'll have uninterrupted privacy tomorrow."

"Are you sure you're not the one trying to avoid me? This is a rather odd hour for a business meeting."

"Not for them. They're on London time, so it's only afternoon." He took her hand and raised it to his lips, lightly kissing her fingertips. His voice was low and suggestive. "Besides, Ms. Conway, I thought you liked serious people."

"Not tonight, I don't. Tonight, I want to be alone with a crazy dreamer who has a thing about trains."

"How about tomorrow morning? With the sunrise over the rockies."

"The sun rises in the east," she pointed out.

"In Aspen, we're surrounded by mountains. The sun rises over one mountain range and sets behind another. The best of everything."

"The top of the world." She recalled the feeling she had while skiing and a soft lassitude overcame her. She yawned. "Go ahead and attend to your business, Jonathan. Sunrise will come soon enough."

Darcy closed her eyes and allowed the subtle whir of the jet engines to lull her into sleep.

When she woke, his two associates had already disembarked. Jonathan was beside her, and she snuggled against his warm chest.

"Sunrise?" she asked lazily.

"Hard to tell. It's overcast and beginning to snow."

She peeked through the porthole window. Huge snowflakes drifted lightly through grey skies, blurring her vision. She returned to her comfortable nest on Jonathan's shoulder. "Looks cold out there."

"Weather reports are calling for a blizzard. Your dear friends, Mr. Scrooge and Mr. Cratchit, have already left for the lodge, and I suppose we ought to follow their example. Unless you'd rather be snowed in on an airplane?"

"No, thank you." She stretched. Though the reclining seat had been comfortable, she wouldn't want to make a habit of sleeping in it. "I seem to remember a king-size bed at your house."

By the time they reached his home, the big flakes

had begun to fall more heavily, swirling the world in white and blanketing the already snowy slopes. Jonathan trundled their suitcases inside and closed the door. "Home, at last."

"At last." She reached up to rake her fingers through his sandy hair. He was still wearing his business suit and camel hair coat. "You must be exhausted."

"Ah yes, the rigorous life of a wheeler-dealer." He slipped his arm around her waist and energetically pulled her against him for a quick kiss. "I'll survive."

"So will I, but after a shower." She grated the palm of her hand against his prickly morning beard and wrinkled her nose. "After you've shaved."

He released her. "You're not having second thoughts, are you? That sounded suspiciously like a rational, practical statement."

"I can't help being sensible—and sensitive—when it comes to rubbing my face against sandpaper. Besides, it must take years of practice to become a full-fledged eccentric." She gazed into his eyes, noting that they were red-rimmed. Though she recognized the sparkle, there was also a weariness. "Jonathan, you look so tired."

"I'll lie down for a minute while you're showering."

She moved toward the brass staircase. "Then, you shave."

"Agreed."

While she was in the shower, Darcy figured that the best thing was to forcibly club him over the head and make him rest. As far as she could determine, he'd been at least twenty-four hours without sleep. Possibly longer. He needed rest.

Of course, she wanted to ravish the man, but she'd prefer for him to be awake during the process. After adjusting the Ace bandage on her wrist, she towel dried her hair, inserted her diaphragm, and wrapped her naked body in her floor-length, navy blue, velour bathrobe.

When she entered the bedroom, she discovered that her plan for knocking him unconscious was unnecessary. In the midst of his book-strewn bedroom, still wearing his clothes, Jonathan had stretched out diagonally across the king-size bed. His eyes were closed and he wasn't moving.

She crept nearer. He'd kicked off his shoes, unbuttoned his vest and his tie was halfway pulled off. Otherwise, he was clad in a very wrinkled pinstriped suit.

This was a different Jonathan than she'd seen before. His aura of energy and tension was gone. His artless pose was vulnerable, touchable. In the innocence of slumber, his chest rose and fell with each regular breath. His lips parted in utter relaxation. His hand curled limply on the brown and gold patterned bedspread.

When she sat beside him on the bed and traced the furrows on his forehead, he stirred, and she immediately withdrew. Very likely, he would be a light sleeper. Running a worldwide business empire meant a demanding schedule. He was probably one of those people who only needed two hours of sleep to function.

Yet he found time for dreams, she remembered, bright fantastic dreams heralded by whistles from long ago trains. Was he dreaming right now? Had he escaped in his mind to that mythical place?

She imagined somewhere like those fairy tale castles on the Rhine with crenelated battlements and a wide moat. Very protected. Very alone. Would she be welcome there? She wondered if the castle walls would be hard and cold, if the great hall would be haunted with drafts. No, she decided. Jonathan's castle would be hung with bright, beautiful tapestries and lit by the warmth of a thousand fires. Jonathan's world.

Rather than disturb him, she tiptoed to the hall linen closet, found a wooly red blanket and returned to drape it over him. When she gently tucked the blanket up to his chin, she was overcome with the desire to kiss him. But then he would surely awaken, and he needed the rest.

Darcy hesitated, chiding herself. Once again, she was being sensible. Considerate and caring, but sensible. Impetuous romance was simply not part of her nature, and for the first time she regretted its lack.

Downstairs, she called her answering service. While she informed her secretary, Karen, that she was out of town and would be unavailable for the rest of the week, she rummaged through Jonathan's kitchen for a snack.

Apparently, his cleaning crew had been at work during his absence because the entire place—apart from a few scattered books in his bedroom—was spotless. The refrigerator had been stocked with cheeses, summer sausage, wine, and vegetables. She closed the refrigerator door. Not hungry. His vulnerable presence haunted her, made her restless, and she couldn't figure out what to do with herself while he was sleeping.

An inspiration struck. She climbed the circular staircase to the bedroom and past the still sleeping Jonathan. She would use these moments to explore the dreamer.

With one tug, the aluminum staircase to the attic slid quietly into place. She ascended to his secret parlor.

Finding the light switch in the semidarkness gave her a problem, and she fumbled before locating the dimmers that regulated the directional light on the symmetrical arrangement of green velvet antique sofas and tables.

She went to the model train. The small metal figures of the handsome 1900s' couple were still standing and waiting for the Twentieth Century Limited. But nothing else had been added or changed.

After a brief search, she discovered the box of metal people and began to unwrap them and carefully place them in appropriate positions. The conductor stood at the ready beside the tracks. She placed a driver in the horse and buggy. More figures took their places on the platform. A switchman posed near the Harbor Creek station.

The process took some time, but Darcy was unaware of the moments. It seemed such a silly thing to do, like playing with dolls, but she was enjoying herself. In another box, she found small houses and buildings that needed some construction. Happily, she arranged the setting, indulging her imagination.

She'd constructed a lovely brownstone house and placed the 1900s' couple outside it. Would they have children? Of course, she decided. She found the figure of a running boy wearing knickers and set him on the sidewalk outside the house, then added a girl jumping rope with a pink bow in her hair.

With each adjustment, she felt closer to Jonathan, as if she were becoming a part of his dream, building upon it. But when she heard his voice, she was startled.

"It looks wonderful," he said. "Thank you, Darcy."

She didn't need to ask if he'd showered and shaved. His sandy hair was still damp. And he was wearing only a towel wrapped around his waist.

Memories of an Aspen Adonis, a hunk, a gorgeous specimen played across her mind. She'd known he was handsome. Jonathan, perfectly impeccable in a tailored suit. Jonathan in his black ski gear. Jonathan sprawled on his bed. And now, Jonathan in a towel. A wicked smile played on her lips. This was her favorite incarnation of Jonathan.

He was magnificent. The directional lighting cast mysterious shadows across his face, and Darcy concentrated on his body. The dark hair sprinkled across his chest narrowed to a suggestive Vee before disappearing beneath the towel. The firm, neatly defined muscularity of his upper body and torso reflected his healthy athleticism. His arms and shoulders rippled with strength as he crossed the room and stood beside her.

With a flick of the button beneath the table, the train whistle sounded and the model of the Twentieth Century Limited jostled to life. She sensed the beginning of a wonderful journey. The final destination was hazy, but for once Darcy was content to go along for the pleasure of the ride.

She watched the model train make its circuit. "Miles to go before they sleep," she said.

He took her shoulders and turned her to face him. "And I have promises to keep. A promise to you, Darcy."

His lips nuzzled her forehead, trailing light kisses on her eyelids, her nose, her lips.

"Let me give you pleasure," he murmured.

But she couldn't hold back, simply could not stand passively and wait. His touch immediately aroused her and she clung to him, consuming his warm naked flesh, drawing the breath from their bodies in a passion-filled kiss.

He gently separated from her, holding her chin in his hand. "I've waited so long for this moment, lady. Let me savor you."

"I'll try." Her limbs trembled with the need for him.

He tugged the velour cord that held her robe in place and unfastened the soft navy blue fabric. With a tantalizing, light caress, he slipped the robe from her shoulders.

The robe fell to the hardwood floor and she stood naked before him. His grey eyes held her in a gaze, almost painful in its intensity, and he gasped. "My God, Darcy, you're perfect."

His hands outlined the curve of her waist and the flare of her hips before he cupped her breasts, teasing the nipples to erection with feathery strokes. "Perfect."

His tender exploration made her feel like the most beautiful woman in the world. He was so rapt in her presence, nearly reverent in his touch.

When she reached for him, he stopped her. "Not yet. I want to see you." He kissed her throat. "To taste you."

"I want you, Jonathan." Her voice was husky. "Now."

Her arms wrapped tightly around his neck and their flesh cleaved together from lips to ankles. Darcy's soft, ivory skin meloed with his chest and flat stomach. His towel had slipped away, and she straddled his leg to massage his hard manhood with her thigh.

She felt herself being lifted, floating, and she wrapped her legs around his body as he carried her, still kissing, to the antique parlor.

When he lowered her to the green velvet sofa, her eyes popped open. "How did we get here?"

"Gossamer wings," he murmured. "Darcy, are you protected?"

"Yes, earlier in the bathroom."

"Good."

She arched herself against him, breathing hard, and he responded with elemental turbulence. His kisses were like fire, sparking her own flame. And they burned together, feeding each other's furor with passion.

When he spread her thighs and entered her, Darcy gave a sharp cry and pulled him close to her. With all her strength, she bucked against him, creating a frenzied rhythm.

Together, they reached the height of fulfillment. She couldn't have imagined such ecstasy until she experienced it. Every fiber of her body was alive. Every nerve ending tingled in harmony with the train whistle from the Lionel model train as it wailed a low, mournful cry.

If these tumultuous sensations were the wages of fantasy, Darcy wished to forever live in a feathery dream state. Softly, gently, she floated back to a reality that would never be the same. Her life was changed by Jonathan's presence.

There wasn't room for both of them to lie on the sofa, so they adjusted to a half-reclining position with Darcy snuggled in his arms.

"What would it be like," she wondered aloud, "to make love in a real sleeping chamber, like this one, rumbling along the railroad tracks in the night."

"We'll have a chance to find out," he said.

"How? In addition to your jets and your limousines, do you also have a time machine?"

"When the Twentieth Century is refurbished, Darcy. There will be a sitting room like this one. And sleeper cars with compartments containing Pullman-style beds."

"A room like this one?" She gave him a teasing poke in the ribs. "Rewriting history? These parlor-type cars were only used on the long, cross-country runs. The Twentieth Century never had a sitting room. It was supposed to be a fast train. Twenty hours from New York to Chicago."

"Actually, there was once a car similar to this attached to the end of the train. A special deluxe parlor for a very special lady and her entourage."

Darcy raised her eyebrows. "And who was this lady?"

"A blue-eyed, black-haired Irish rose." He traced a line along her flank and over her hip. "Your great-grandmother, Nell Conway."

Darcy caught his questing hand and brought it to

her lips. These moments with him were so sweet, poignant with history. Of all her family, Darcy most resembled the lovely Nell. She doubted, however, that her great-grandmother had ever been in a similar position with a man. "Tell me more about your dream train, Jonathan."

"As you would know if you'd paid attention at the meetings I've had with your father and aunt, the renewed Twentieth Century will be a luxury passenger express. The old-fashioned sitting room will be for private parties and meetings. Or open to the public with a bar and bartender stationed at the far room."

She felt left out. She hadn't listened at the meetings. In fact, she'd avoided attending them whenever possible. And their plans seemed to have progressed considerably. "How far along are you?"

"I hope to schedule the maiden run—that's the test—for April the first."

"April Fool's Day?" She laughed. "You beautiful fool. How on earth are you going to accomplish that in less than two months?"

"This will be for limited service. A maiden run with only six Pullman cars available. I don't plan to open the train to the public until June fifteenth."

"Of course," she said. "The anniversary of the inaugural run of the Twentieth Century Limited. June fifteenth, 1902."

"There's only one thing that worries me, Darcy, and that's your father's idea about making a public appearance at the maiden run. Of course, I'd planned to be there, but incognito.''

''Sunglasses and a fake moustache,'' she said with a chuckle.

''I do have something like that,'' he sheepishly admitted. ''It's a beard and round-framed glasses and a poorly fitted tweed suit. The absent-minded professor look.''

It didn't surprise her that he would choose a professor for his alter ego. With all the books in his bedroom, he must be nearly educated enough for a doctorate. Self-educated, she remembered. He'd told her that he'd dropped out of school in seventh grade. Self-educated. Self-made. No wonder he had the reputation of being a loner. Darcy smiled. She knew the vast inaccuracy of that description. Jonathan was warm, giving, and wonderful.

They lay together quietly for a moment, then Darcy wriggled. ''This isn't really comfortable, you know.''

''I don't expect the Victorians intended it for the use we've put it to.''

''I don't expect so.''

He nuzzled her hair and whispered. ''Shall we go downstairs to the king-size bed?''

''Move into the present?'' She arched back her neck at a severe angle and kissed his chin.

He traced the line of her throat. ''I guess there are some present day conveniences—like king-size beds—that are improvements on the good, old days.''

"Indeed, there are. And I'm a very modern woman."

When he crossed the room to turn off the Lionel train, his gaze rested on the 1900s' handsome couple standing outside their brownstone with two children playing nearby. His grey eyes twinkled as he glanced at Darcy. "I see our couple has made some progress. Are they married now?"

"Oh yes." She unselfconsciously joined him. Being naked had never felt so right before. "Married with two children. And I think the kids are named Amanda and Harvey, after Paul Harvey who brought fine dining to the railroads."

"And our handsome couple? What are their names?"

"I'll leave that to your overactive imagination."

After another promising kiss, they descended the stairs. Darcy had just settled on the king-size bed when the telephone rang.

"I have to answer," he said apologetically. "This system never puts through calls unless it's an emergency."

"I understand."

It was rather complimentary, she thought. His worldwide empire was held at bay by her presence. Their lovemaking took precedence over million dollar corporate decisions, the rise and collapse of entire economic systems.

He held out the telephone. "It's for you. Your cousin."

Darcy took the phone. "Paula?"

"Hi, darling. Nice to have you back in Aspen."

"How on earth did you get this number?"

"Well, darling, since you were too rude to give me anything more than Jonathan's dumb answering service, I called your father in Chicago."

Darcy looked questioningly at Jonathan. "You gave my father your private, emergency number?"

Jonathan nodded. "He has a lot of emergencies and he drives the answering services crazy when they don't put him right through."

She shook her head and returned her attention to Paula. "So, cousin, how's the love affair of the century going?"

"Which one? Darling, I've been through two others since you met my knight in shining, and you simply will not believe what has happened to me. I've actually taken up skiing and I love it." She paused. "Almost as much as I enjoy the gorgeous Nordic types who continually offer to be my private instructors."

"Uh-huh," Darcy murmured as she watched Jonathan stretch his long, lean body beside hers on the bed.

"And, Darcy, I haven't had my hair done in a week. Or my nails. And I have one of those funny raccoon-eye ski tans. Honestly, if the ladies at the GCC could see me, they'd never believe it."

"The GCC?" Darcy vaguely questioned. Jonathan

had inched the covers down and was drawing slow, tantalizing circles round her breasts.

"Greater Chicago Charities," Paula said.

"Of course." It seemed so long ago since she and Paula had argued in her ransacked office about the GCC luncheon. A million years ago, before she knew Jonathan. Another lifetime. He lowered his lips to her breast, and she gasped with pleasure.

"Darcy?"

"I have to go." Darcy hesitated. Something was not right about this phone call. "Paula, how did you happen to know I was here?"

"Everybody knows. That's really why I called. Two men checked into the lodge early this morning, and they've been talking up a storm about Jonathan Hillcroft and his ladyfriend—Ms. Conway, if you please. Not only that, I've seen these two men making phone calls."

Darcy remembered the two executives from London on the plane. "What have they been saying?"

"It runs something along the line of: Jonathan Hillcroft is a reclusive ass and he lives in Aspen. Their information is complete with Jonathan's address. If there weren't a blizzard outside, I'm sure you'd have reporters camped on your doorstep at this very moment."

Darcy thanked her cousin and rang off.

"Jonathan, how did your negotiations on the plane turn out?"

"Not very well, I'm afraid. I had to turn down their proposal."

Her eyelids drooped, trying to hide the information. But she had to tell him. His quiet haven was about to be turned into a public show. His privacy—and hers—was about to be lost. "It seems that Mr. Scrooge and Mr. Cratchit are getting even."

EIGHT

Their idyll had ended too soon.

Jonathan's response to Paula's information was angry and immediate. "We'll have to leave," he told Darcy.

"We can't. There's a blizzard outside." She smoothed his brow. "It'll be hours before anyone comes out in this weather."

"Never underestimate the press."

He gazed into her china blue eyes. She was perfect, so delicate, such a lady. He hated to expose her to sordid, rude questions from reporters who would undoubtedly link their names in the most sleazy fashion. "You'll have to excuse me, Darcy. I need to make a couple of phone calls."

"It's okay. You get on the phone, and I'll scavenge some food from the kitchen."

She rose from the bed and went to his closet, selecting one of his soft wool Pendleton shirts in a green and grey plaid. "May I borrow this?"

"I'd like it very much if you did."

The shirt fell almost to her knees. She rolled up the sleeves. "Very nice. It smells like you."

"And that's good?"

"It's wonderfully sexy."

No more sexy than she was. Desire urged him to rise from the bed and take her into his arms, to cover her body with kisses. But there was a situation to be dealt with. When she disappeared down the circular staircase to the first floor, he rose from the bed and pulled on a pair of Levis and another Pendleton shirt.

First, he contacted his trusted local employees, ordering them to put the lid on the disgruntled London executives and to discourage reporters as best they could. From their responses, he knew that the damage had already been done.

It wasn't fair, dammit. Aspen was a small town populated by celebrities. Movie stars and politicians and best-selling authors stood on every street corner. Why on earth should they bother with him?

Jonathan knew the answer. He was caught in a web of his own spinning. If he hadn't enforced such stringent policies to protect his privacy, he would not have been so appealing to the media. If he'd issued a biography, even full of lies, the mystique would be gone.

He dialed the offices of Bill Randall, head of promotion at Jonathan's main branch in Sunnyvale, California.

"We have a publicity leak in Aspen," Jonathan said. "And there is a lady involved. Ms. Darcy Conway."

"Yes, Jonathan?"

"I want no mention of her name in any gossip column. Is that clear?"

"I'll do my best, but—

"She is a friend. I am transacting business with her family." He paused. "Maybe you can turn this problem into profit. Try to divert attention to the Twentieth Century Limited project. Mention the pleasures of railway travel, emphasize luxury, adventure, the unfortunate need to subsidize Amtrak with taxpayers' monies, etcetera."

"Jonathan? The situation would be most easily defused if you would consent to a press conference."

"You never give up, do you? Well, Randy, you've about worn me down. If you handle this problem well, I'll consider it."

Jonathan hung up the telephone. Randall was correct; a press conference would halt rumors. But Jonathan couldn't bring himself to do it. The very thought of laying his past before the world unnerved him.

A familiar coldness seeped through his limbs. He shook it off and placed a local call to a friend who sometimes worked for him as a bodyguard. In a moment, Jonathan had arranged for three men to be subtly posed outside his house.

He notified his executive secretary of the situation.

He called the pilot of his private jet, informing him to standby for takeoff as soon as the weather improved.

"Where to?" the pilot asked.

"I'll let you know."

There wasn't a destination far enough away. Despite his wealth and power, Jonathan realized that Darcy's caution was correct: He could not fly away from his past.

Years ago, he had submitted to a meeting with the press and had endured the resulting, tawdry stories that described him as sad, little Jonathan Hillcroft who had struggled through such a poverty-stricken childhood. Abandoned by his father. Orphaned at age twelve when his mother died. Homeless. Selling oranges on street corners.

He clenched his fist and smote the pillows behind his head. He did not need the world's pity. He would not be held up as a symbol of poor boy makes good. Yes, there had been obstacles. Yes, he had overcome them. But that didn't make him a hero.

Heroes had puffed-up chests, suitable for pinning medals upon. Jonathan was shy. More than anything else, he hated speaking in public. And it wasn't necessary, not with the meticulous way he had arranged his life. He was perfectly content to hide his embarrassing shyness behind a cold facade. Damn those blabbing executives anyway.

He calmed as Darcy came up the staircase, carefully balancing two heavy ceramic mugs, croissants, and cheeses on a wooden tray. She was so lovely. Like a porcelain doll. "You're a finely bred woman, Darcy."

"Like an AKC certified canine?"

He laughed. "I can't help admiring you."

She set the tray on the bed and presented him a steaming brew of Irish coffee topped with frothy whipped cream. "Have you taken care of your business?"

"As well as I can. I'm afraid we'll have to stay here until the storm lets up, then it's best to take off." He took a sip of his coffee and sighed. "It's unfortunate. I know you wanted to go skiing."

She wiped a trace of whipped cream from his upper lip and slipped her finger through her own lips to lick it off. "In the immortal words of my cousin, Paula. I think we can find several pleasurable alternatives to skiing."

He took the cup from her hand and placed it on the bedside table before pulling her down beside him on the pillows. "Do you care to show me what you have in mind?"

"I'd be delighted."

In contrast to their earlier storm of passion, Darcy lingered over his body. Slowly and thoroughly, she explored his muscular physique, the fascinating texture of his hair and his lips. She especially adored his lips, their taste and fullness, their skill in arousal.

Likewise, he discovered the most tender parts of

her body. His lips paid fond tribute to her breasts. His hands massaged the curve of her waist and splayed across the swell of her firm buttocks. He learned a new meaning for pleasure at the honeyed juncture of her thighs.

Their lovemaking transported them to a mythical place where dreams became reality, and truth was ever so sweet.

In the afterglow as she lay beside him, sipping cooled Irish coffee, she asked, "Why not face them, Jonathan? The reporters. Why not tell them who you are and what you're like?"

"Like this?" He indicated the tangled sheets and the disarrayed covers half-drawn over their bodies.

She snuggled against his shoulder. "Really, Jonathan. Why not tell them?"

"I wouldn't know where to begin. I've had a tangled life. Streetfights and struggles. I've known a lot of people, some good and several not so good. Many of them never heard of your Auntie Lou's social register."

"Dear me," she said, pretending to be haughtily offended. "You mean you aren't one of the Boston Hales?"

"My real name isn't even Hillcroft."

"It's not?"

"It is now. Early on in my checkered career, I had it legally changed. And it did make a difference for me. When I dropped my old name, I dropped a load of my past. I felt like I could redefine myself."

"Makes sense. In fact, it sounds unusually practical for you." She smiled up at him. "What was your name before?"

"I'd rather not say."

"Please, we shouldn't have secrets."

He winced. "When I was growing up my name was Jonathan Frederick Hogswindler."

She suppressed a giggle. "Hillcroft is definitely better."

"I thought so, too. In any case, my past is buried, cemented over with years. I don't want to bring it to light."

"But it might save you trouble in the long run."

"Darcy, you can't possibly understand. You were bred and born a lady."

"A lady?" She rolled her eyes. "In some ways, you're still stuck in the early 1900s, Jonathan. Class differences are as outdated as male chauvinism. I am a woman."

"I won't argue with that, but you know what I mean. Your life was sheltered, beautifully cocooned. Charmed and charming. And that's the way life ought to be. In a perfect world, there would be no poverty, no fear, no shame."

"I've felt fear, Jonathan. And shame. You don't have a monopoly on tragedy." She drew away from him, stung by his lack of understanding. "Everyone assumes that if you come from a wealthy family, you can't possibly have problems. Not *real* problems. And that's so wrong. Believe me, I've lived it. I've seen it. Beautiful, rich women so tortured by despair that they've committed suicide. Is their hurt less real because they can afford a manicure? Is their death less painful?"

"You've made your point, Darcy."

"Of all people, I would expect you to understand. You're one of the richest men in the world. Yet, right now, you're a prisoner in your own expensive abode, as surely as if you were in jail. Is your frustration less real?"

"No," he said quietly.

A silent moment passed between them, allowing this difference to settle uneasily. It was difficult for Jonathan to shed his lifelong fantasies about "old money." He wanted to put her on a pedestal, but she kept knocking out the supports.

She glanced toward the window. "The snow is beginning to let up."

He gave a long sigh. "Yes, it is."

"Let's not wait here for them, Jonathan. Let's ski."

He regarded her with amusement. Obviously, she had never been a target of a media attack when papparrazzi flocked like a nasty breed of pigeons—a cross between pigeons and vultures.

"Think about it," she said. "If we're out on the slopes, all bundled up and wearing goggles, no one can distinguish us from the other skiers."

He considered her logic and accepted it. One ski run might be worth the risk if they could escape from the house before anyone saw them. "Let's do it, then."

By the time they'd changed into their gear, the snowfall had lessened to a sputter. When they crept through the six inches of newly fallen snow to the garage, no one was lying in wait for them.

"I was right," Darcy said triumphantly. "Nobody's around."

"Would you care to know why?"

He turned and waved. Instantly, two very large shadows materialized from either side of the house to return his greeting. "Number three is watching the back door," he said. "My friendly neighborhood bodyguards."

She took Jonathan's arm and whispered, "Were they watching the house while we were making love?"

He ushered her into the passenger side of the Bronco. "Yes, they were."

She shivered. "That's creepy. But it's kind of exotic, too. Like spies and international intrigues. You really don't have any privacy, do you?"

"No, I don't." He eased the engine into gear. "Ready to ski? Are you sure your wrist is okay?"

Her doctor in Chicago had given her an air cast, a metal brace that attached with velcro strips. She thunked the metal with her gloved right hand. "This is probably the only part of my body that wouldn't be injured in a fall. The bionic wrist."

Jonathan drove slowly over the snowy roads

toward the ski lifts. After a few blocks, he noticed that a Jeep seemed to be tailing them. A reporter, he thought, grudgingly giving the Jeep driver high marks for persistence before he took a hard right and watched in the rearview mirror as the Jeep spun in a one hundred and eighty degree turn on the deceptively icy road.

Darcy clung to her seat belt. "What are you doing?"

"We were being followed."

She peered over her shoulder at the still circling Jeep. Her tone was sardonic. "Next time, warn me before you pull any kind of secret agent stunt."

"I didn't want to worry you."

"I would prefer being worried to not knowing."

He parked and whipped their skis off the rack. Only a few other intrepid skiers were braving the weather. Jonathan and Darcy passed quickly through the lift line. On the ride to the top, they snuggled together, sharing body warmth.

"I wonder if it's possible to make love on a chair lift," she said. "Without the skiis, of course."

"Of course." He nudged her knit wool cap aside and nibbled at her ear. "But there's no point in considering it."

"Why not? Too cold for you?"

"No protection," he said.

She laughed. "Does that mean you're not ready to start your own little brood of Hogswindlers?"

The thought of children had crossed his mind.

Their children, his and Darcy's, beautiful children with her black hair and blue eyes. Still, he said, "Not just yet."

As she cuddled against him, he felt an excitement stirring within her, a building of emotion. He was beginning to recognize her moods, not to necessarily understand them, but to know when her temper had been engaged. Or when she was hurt. Or when she felt mischievous.

"Tell me about the Twentieth Century Limited," she said.

"Yeah," he shivered. "It's going to be air conditioned. And heated. Really warm."

"I want to help with the planning for it."

He kissed her cold nose. What was that old saying? Cold nose, warm heart? Or was that for dogs? "I'd like that very much, Darcy. Do you think you can stand working that closely with your father and aunt?"

She hadn't considered that. Myopically, she'd imagined the Twentieth Century project to be solely Jonathan. Long, late nights together. Planning and dreaming.

Close association with Poppa and Auntie Lou might be a giant step backwards in her life and career. After all, she'd finally managed to move her offices out of the family home, and Thomas Wolfe had said it succinctly: You can't go home again.

But she wanted to work with Jonathan, to watch

him operate. Maybe this would be a case of taking one step back and three forward. "I'll risk it."

"That's great," he said warmly. "Which area do you want to focus on? I should warn you that your aunt has dibs on menu planning. And your mother has presented some attractive ideas for decor."

"Fine. I'll leave the women's work to them." She grinned wickedly. "I want to be in charge of publicity."

"From that gleam in your eyes, I suppose this means I'm going to be wearing a neon sandwich board sign that says: Ride the Twentieth Century and Meet the Reclusive Billionaire."

She grinned. "Do you want my help or not?"

"I'll chance it. Darcy Conway, welcome aboard."

She tightened her embrace. "Full steam ahead!"

When they dismounted the chairlift, Jonathan instructed her. "Stay with me. We're going left."

She nodded. It was really cold. Freezing, frigid cold. The wind slashed snow into her face as she aimed her skis toward the wide slope he'd indicated. When she pulled up parallel to him on the slope to catch her breath, Darcy planted her poles in the snow and swung her hands vigorously, circulating the blood and warming her fingers.

He raised his pole and pointed to another skier at the top of the slope. "Here comes your first project, Publicity Lady. I think he's the guy from the Jeep."

"I thought you lost him."

"Even James Bond slips up occasionally. Anyway, this guy made a point of pushing onto the chair behind us. I'd hoped we'd get away from him up here, but he seems to be an expert skier.''

The skier waved to them and shouted, ''Hey, you. Wait up.''

''No problem,'' Darcy said. ''Would you rather race to the bottom or face the music?''

''Neither.'' He didn't want to take the risk of speed skiing, not with Darcy's recent injury. Though she'd assured him about her bionic wrist, he did not wish to be responsible for her being hurt again. ''But, dammit, I guess we're going to have to talk our way out of this.''

Darcy licked her lips. ''My pleasure. Let me handle this. Kind of a pre-employment test.''

There was determination in her set, little jaw, and an impish light from her blue eyes. ''You're going to like this, aren't you?''

''I might not be a world class dreamer, Jonathan, but I can handle a practical joke.''

When the other skier joined them, swishing to a snow-spraying stop, Jonathan almost felt sorry for the man. Darcy was prepared to chop him into mincemeat, and to enjoy herself while she did it.

Before he could speak, she snapped, ''You can park it right there, mister. Just who do you think you are?''

'Peter Benowski of the Denver *Herald*, financial page.'' He looked around Darcy to Jonathan. ''When

I heard you were here, Hillcroft, I couldn't believe it. How about an interview?''

"Hold it," Darcy snarled. "You don't have clearance.''

"Clearance? What are you talking about?''

"I'd advise you to move it, Benowski. Real quick. We're expecting a V.I.S. to come through here momentarily.''

"V.I.S.?''

"Very Important Skier," she said. "You are aware that a former President of the U.S. lives down the road in Vail.''

"Sure, but—''

"Clear out, buddy." She paused. "Benowski? Is that a Russian name?''

"I don't get this. Are you supposed to be CIA?''

"GCC," Darcy said. "And don't bother asking for I.D. because we're so far undercover that we don't carry any. Isn't that right?" She turned to Jonathan. "Agent Hogswindler.''

"Yes, Agent Irish." He bit the inside of his cheeks to keep from laughing.

"Hey, it's too cold to play games," the reporter said, turning to Jonathan. "Hillcroft, I want a comment on your proposed South African diamond mines.''

"That's it," Darcy said. She pulled back her parka to reveal the metal brace of her cast and spoke into it. "This is Irish. We have an individual who refuses to leave the slopes. A suspected red agent.''

"What are you doing?" he demanded.

"Making contact with the snipers we have placed in strategic positions in the spruce trees." She pulled her parka back into place. "Sorry, Benowski. I can't be responsible for what happens to you."

"Lady, you are one crazy broad."

"Am I? Listen, Benowski, if this really was Hillcroft, do you think he'd be out here on the slopes without his bodyguards? From what I understand, he's nutty enough and rich enough to put snipers in the trees himself."

"She's right," Jonathan said. "If I were Hillcroft, I would certainly not venture out unprotected."

"Indeed," Darcy added. "He could probably raise his pinky, and twenty former pro linebackers would come skiing after you like you were a pigskin on the five yard line."

Benowski glanced toward the trees, frowned, and pushed away from them. "I'll get you for this, Hillcroft."

As the reporter skied away, Jonathan burst into laughter. "The snipers in the spruce? Protecting a V.I.S.? The GCC?"

"Greater Chicago Charities," she said primly. "Paula is the vice president. And it worked. So, do I have the job as head of publicity?"

"You got it." Still laughing, he pulled her close and kissed her frozen nose. "I didn't know you were such a crazy broad."

"Must be genetic."

They pushed off and skied through the bitter, wintry cold. Jonathan stayed behind her, keeping a careful eye on her movements. Her controlled style pleased him, but when she tucked down to fly over a mogul near the base of the mountain, he was excited by her daring. She was a strange mixture: One moment, she was cool and practical. The next, she was emotional and hot as a blue butane flame. But always, no matter how much she denied it, she was a lady.

At the ski lift, they took a sharp veer to the right, toward the parking area and managed to evade the waiting Benowski. Safe in the Bronco, they headed toward the airport.

The sky had cleared enough for takeoff and soon they were airborn. Their destination was Chicago.

Darcy settled into the highback reclining chair and smiled up at him when he took the seat beside her and presented her with a corned beef on rye sandwich and a tulip glass of imported German beer.

When she lifted her sandwich, she noticed a coiled glitter on the plate. A necklace. She held the gold chain and a pendant of heart shaped diamonds with a tiny locomotive engine bursting through the middle. "Thank you, Jonathan, this is lovely."

"Happy Valentine's Day."

"Is it? I'd forgotten."

A tear of happiness welled in her eyes. His sweet gesture touched a secretly romantic place within her that had been dormant for years, perhaps forever.

She blinked, struggling for control. "I don't have anything for you."

"Yes, Darcy, you do." He wiped away the single tear that spilled down her cheek. "The wonderful gift of yourself."

Their lips pressed lightly together in confirmation of an unspoken commitment.

Jonathan fumbled as he fastened the pendant necklace around her throat, and Darcy wondered if he was as uncomfortable as she was with the unguarded sentimentality that was growing between them.

She bit into the sandwich he'd made for her. It wasn't delicious, kind of cardboard-tasting without mustard, but she was so hungry she would have eaten escargot. She washed it down with a sip of frothy beer. "Did you make this sandwich yourself?"

He nodded.

"Well, it's a good thing you're rich," she said. "If you had to feed yourself, you'd die of indigestion."

"Not me. I'd find myself a sweet, little woman who could cook."

"You sexist Hogswindler."

"But I know how to make a lady happy," he teased. "If I weren't rich, I wouldn't have anything to offer to another guy."

"Double sexist." She sipped her beer.

His lips curled in a wide grin. "You can't cook, either. Can you?"

"Let me put it to you this way. When I was in boarding school, we had scullery duty two days a week. Peeling potatoes, mixing batter, things like that.'' She paused. ''I accidentally set fire to the kitchen. Twice.''

He discarded his sandwich and slipped his arm around her shoulders. ''I guess we're both lucky that I'm rich.''

''I'm luckier.'' She swallowed the last bite of corned beef. ''I get the benefit, i.e., you know how to please a woman. Without the scullery work.''

''Somehow, Darcy, you make everything sound like a contract.''

''That's not such a bad thing. For example . . .'' She touched the diamond pendant. ''You give to me.'' She unfastened the first button on his shirt and placed a light kiss in the hollow of his throat. ''And I give to you.''

''I like this contract.'' He glided his fingertips to her waist and burrowed under her lavender turtleneck, past her smooth belly to her breast. Her taut nipple pressed against the fine lace of her brassiere.

She flipped up the arm rest between their seats and eased herself onto his lap. Holding his face in both her hands, she kissed him lightly, then harder. Her tongue slipped between his teeth.

Together, they created a turbulence in the sky that had nothing to do with weather conditions. Before they touched down at Chicago's Midway Airfield, Darcy had learned what it was like to make love, ten thousand feet in the air.

NINE

Darcy's office building was made of tinted grey glass, a vast expanse of non-glaring glass from the tenth story to the first floor bank. Darcy admired the clean precision of the structure. Razor-straight lines cut efficiently through the cloudy suburban skies and reflected them at the same time. Very modern, she thought, though it was occasionally disconcerting to be so visible.

Five weeks after Valentine's Day, she stood at her window on the fifth floor, looking down on budding but still barren treetops. If March went out like a lamb, she told herself, the view would soon be marvelous. The crocus and iris were already poking through the earth. But right now it looked chilly and drab. Even the up-scale shopping mall across the street seemed dismal with a tacky red "Sale" sign in the window of an exclusive boutique.

Her secretary, Karen, who was proving to be a gem, tapped on the door and entered. "Darcy, your father is on line one."

"Thank you." She went to her desk and pressed the button on her white telephone. "Hi, Poppa."

"Don't you 'hi, Poppa' me, young lady."

"Bye, Poppa?" she said hopefully.

"I won't be served chicken on the Twentieth Century Limited," he said. "Railroads and cattle, that's the ticket. Railroads and cattle go hand-in-hand."

"Or hoof-in-mouth," she muttered under her breath. "I thought we decided that the menu would include both."

"I don't like the chickens. It's sissy food. You'd better tell Jonathan that when he comes calling today."

"I will, Poppa."

"Good." He hung up.

Darcy turned to Karen. "Six more days until that stupid train makes its maiden run. Maybe then, we'll have some quiet and sanity around here."

"Speaking of the train," Karen said as she apologetically held out a handful of yellow Western Union telegrams, "these are from your Aunt Louisa."

Darcy glanced through the stack of telegrams. Unlike her father who was likely to call anyone at any time, her Auntie Lou had always mistrusted telephones. In her opinion, the only civilized communication was via the postal service. Or telegram. Each Western Union message listed another person or family that Auntie Lou wished to invite to the maiden run of the Twentieth Century. Thus far in the arrangements, her list of suggested invitees ran almost as long as the Chicago area telephone book.

Darcy passed the telegrams back to Karen. "Would you please log these under Possibles."

"But the invitations went out weeks ago."

"Over two hundred," she confirmed, "not including invitations to the press. Auntie Lou can't seem to grasp that concept."

"Which reminds me," Karen said. "Some of the R.S.V.P.'s are coming here. Should I tell anyone that Jonathan is going to be there?"

"Let's keep that quiet for right now." Darcy picked up a file folder from her desk. "Karen, please put through a call to Mrs. Archibald. I need to speak with her today or tomorrow."

"Consider it done." She left the room.

Darcy perched on the edge of her desk chair and stared at the model train on her desk. *The Little Engine That Could.* The closer they got to the first journey for the Twentieth Century, the more she identified with the over-burdened little train.

Her idea to work on publicity had backfired spectacularly. She'd expected the shared interest to solidify her relationship with Jonathan. Instead, because of her efficient management, he was able to spend more time out of town on his regular business.

And Darcy was left alone to deal with the outrageous demands from her family who had taken the resurrection of the Twentieth Century to heart. Not only was she battling with her father and Auntie Lou, but her brother from Seattle had gotten involved and two distant cousins and four aunts and uncles. She'd had to limit the number of Conways invited to the maiden run to thirty-five.

She touched the diamond pendant Jonathan had given her and smiled. He would be here today. At least she hoped he would be here. During the past five weeks, she'd only seen him eight times. And there had been four other cancellations. On a rational level, she could understand that he'd been snowed in at New York and that certain negotiations had run longer than expected. But her emotional response ranged from screaming red rage to the depths of the blues.

Karen tapped lightly on the door to Darcy's office again.

"Come in."

Her secretary was beaming. "You have a visitor."

Jonathan, behind a gigantic display of red roses, sauntered through the door, and Karen discretely closed it behind him.

Darcy bolted from her chair. As soon as he placed the fragrant bouquet on her credenza, she flung her arms around his neck and kissed him. He enthusiastically returned her kiss and her embrace, swirling her off the floor in a wide, joyous circle. Her red pumps that matched the stripe in her grey plaid suit fell off.

In his presence, she always felt tousled and happily disarrayed.

"Put me down, you animal."

"Admit it, woman. You love it."

She hugged him more tightly. "Indeed, I do."

"I've missed you, Darcy."

"I've been right here, keeping the engines stoked. You're the one who's always flying off into the wild, blue yonder."

"Business," he said.

"I'm beginning to hate that word."

She couldn't stop smiling. There were a million things she ought to be telling him, but her pleasure at seeing him again erased every last detail. "Thank you for the roses. They're gorgeous."

"I thought you needed some color in this office."

"What's wrong with my office?"

"As offices go, it's great," he said. "Lots of blonde wood, clean lines, and conservative color scheme of grey and blue. But it doesn't entirely suit you."

"Right," she scoffed. "Because I'm so flamboyant."

His eyes slid over her neat, plaid suit with its wide, red leather belt and grey silk blouse. He stroked the Vee neckline of her blouse, sending tremors through her body. Then he kissed her again. "Lady, you are more exotic than you know."

As she rested her cheek against his clean smelling cotton shirt, she gazed through the huge glass window—exposed for all the world to see and she didn't care. Her fingers toyed with the end of his striped tie. "I'm not exotic," she said. "You're the one with the wild dreams and crazy fantasies."

Jonathan was also looking toward the floor-to-ceiling tinted window. "People who live in glass offices, Darcy, shouldn't throw stones."

"I do have one fantasy," she murmured. "That you'll stay in town for a month."

"Sorry. I'm only here for a day. Then back to California for two more days. Then I'm here until the maiden run." He held her tightly and gave a deep sigh. "And I guess we need to talk about the train."

She knew which train he meant—the Twentieth Century Limited. And she heartily resented it. She had only one day to spend with him, and half of that time would probably be consumed with train business. "Only a day," she said, trying to keep the pleading note from her voice. "Twenty-four teensy-weensy hours?"

"Maybe thirty."

"Then I propose a contract. Only twenty-five percent of our time will be spent on the train. The rest is for me."

"I never thought you'd prefer romance to business."

"Before I met you, Jonathan, I never knew what fun romance could be."

The intercom on Darcy's desk buzzed.

Darcy groaned before she answered: "Yes, Karen?"

"Sorry to disturb you, Darcy. But Mrs. Archibald returned your call. And she sounds very upset."

"Thank you. I'll take the call."

Darcy pushed the button for line one and said, "Mrs. Archibald? Darcy Conway. How are you today?"

The voice that came through the telephone receiver sounded very old and very tired. "I can't meet the payment, dear. So, I'm afraid, I shall have to lose my Renoir."

"But I thought your son's business was doing so well."

"Last month, he made several bad decisions. For his company, it was worse than Black Tuesday. He lost almost everything."

"Let's consider alternatives, Mrs. Archibald."

Darcy sank into the chair behind her desk. This was terrible! Sweet, elderly Mrs. Archibald had gone through Original Property Brokers to secure a $1.6 million loan for her son's stock brokerage business. Her collateral was an original Renoir. Not only was the artwork beautiful, but it had emotional significance as well. The ballerina painting had been a gift from her late husband. He presented it forty years ago when Mrs. Archibald retired from her career as a professional dancer. The elderly lady was now crippled by arthritis.

Darcy had, in fact, discouraged the loan when she saw how sadly Mrs. Archibald signed the papers.

The loss of her Renoir would be the loss of her beautiful memories.

Darcy scanned the thick file folder on the Archibald transaction. It included a detailed prospectus on her son's business and his personal worth. He'd been successful in repaying one hundred thousand dollars per quarter for the past year, and Darcy simply could not conceive of how his company had floundered so badly.

She noted with a groan that the investor who had loaned the money was Ken Terrence, a voracious art collector, whose desire for the valuable and prestigious Renoir would make him particularly difficult to deal with.

The terms indicated that Mrs. Archibald had reached the end of her grace period. By April first, she had to repay one-hundred thousand dollars against the loan. Or forfeit the painting.

"I'm looking at my Renoir right now," Mrs. Archibald said wistfully. "Do you think Mr. Terrence would allow me to come and see it sometimes?"

"You will not lose your painting," Darcy said. "I'll negotiate with your son and with Mr. Terrence. I'm sure something can be worked out."

She rang off. Her hand rested on the telephone as she sadly met Jonathan's gaze. "I have a horrible premonition that this won't work out. Terrence has been lusting after that painting since the beginning of this transaction."

"Tell me about it."

She lay back in her swivel chair and sketched the details for him. "Any ideas?"

"You don't think Terrence will give her more time?"

"Of course, I'll try him. But the outlook is not good."

"And the son?" Jonathan asked.

"I don't understand how he could fall apart like that. But, of course, the stock market has been so volatile. Only a few missteps and bam!"

"I do have a solution," Jonathan offered. He took his flat wallet from his suit coat pocket and flipped through his stack of thousand dollar bills.

Darcy laughed. "Not even you, Jonathan. Not even you carry a hundred thousand dollars in your pocket."

"I have on occasion, but I'm a little depleted from my trip to Amsterdam."

"I've wondered since the first time we met, why you carry so much cash."

He sat on the edge of her desk and leaned toward her. "It's a long story."

"I love your long stories." She did. One of her favorite things was to lie beside him in the intimate dark and listen as he rambled on with tales about his recent escapades in high finance and anecdotes about his wild past.

"This particular bad habit started when I was nineteen," he said. "I had a partner. A guy who was considerably older and wiser than I was. In one year, he taught me more about business than an MBA could learn in a lifetime. The secrets of distribution, marketing, negotiating. But he had a weakness. He loved to bet on the ponies. During the year of our association, I let him hold all the money I earned. Like a bank, he said.''

"And he kept it?"

"Not intentionally. I believed him when he said that he always meant to hold my share separate. But somehow when he got to the racing track, my money jumped through the betting window right along with his. He told me about it at the end of a year. And he made it into a lesson. Never put all your money where you can't keep an eye on it. Banks can close. Property can be devastated in a natural disaster. There's no sure thing except a bit of green in your pocket.''

He counted out twenty thousand dollars and set it on her desk. "This is a start for your negotiations with Terrence.''

"I can't take that, Jonathan.''

"Sure you can. Put me on your list of investors.''

She pushed the money back toward him. "No. This is my business and my problem. I won't have you bailing me out.''

"Fine, Darcy. Handle the money any way you want, but it's yours. In any case, I wouldn't mind being on your investor list. I'm sure you occasionally run across properties that I would be interested in.''

"The properties are only collateral,'' she said.

"This would be the first time I've lost one to the investor."

"That's an outstanding record."

"You bet it is. If only it didn't have to fall apart with Mrs. Archibald's Renoir."

She left her desk and stood at the floor-to-ceiling window, looking down at the budding oak trees. Not only was she worried about losing the painting, but this wasn't the way she wanted to be with Jonathan. Fierce independence was a fine trait, but not in a romantic relationship. With Jonathan, she wanted to be soft, vulnerable, even exotic.

"I've struggled with this business for seven years," she said. "It's taken that long for it to make sense, to be profitable."

"Not true. I'm sure you remember those market studies I had done on you? Original Property Brokers was profitable within three months."

"Sure, I made enough to scrape by. But now I'm doing well, really well. I'm successful. I have my own money for investment."

More than the hard work, Original Property Brokers had been a mainstay in her life, a shelter against her family's eccentricity, a tangible asset she could build upon. Throughout the rise and fall of her affair with Thomas O'Bannion, she'd depended on long hours of work to keep her sanity. When she had to pull her family out of financial crisis, her business had withstood the need. She depended upon it. Needed it.

Yet as she gazed through the window of her glass house, her work seemed as barren as the still leafless trees. Her voice trembled. "Why don't I care about it anymore? Half the time, I feel like a cheap pawnbroker."

He came up behind her and wrapped his arms around her waist. "Everyone feels like that from time to time, Darcy. Being self-employed is tough."

"I can handle being tough. Hard work doesn't upset me. But this feeling is different." She leaned against his chest. "I have this idiotic urge to dump the whole thing. To burn all my expensive, neat suits. Jonathan, I've even wanted to learn how to cook."

"Wow, that does sound unnatural."

"Don't tease. It is bizarre for me. Ever since you came into my life, I've been doing things that make no sense. Dealing with my family, actually listening to their crazy ideas. My mind drifts off during nego- tiations. I've been daydreaming." She shuddered. "All my life, I've been practical and controlled. I've hated every evidence of irresponsibility. And now, it seems like I'm behaving like one of them. A kooky Conway."

"You're yourself, Darcy. A lovely contradiction."

She spun around and faced him. "I want to come with you on your trips. To give up my work and fly away with you. To be there when you get home. To make a home. For us."

"I wouldn't say no, Darcy." His grey eyes were

serious and concerned. "Is that what you really want?"

"Yes."

"Then take the twenty thousand dollars I offered you."

"No."

She couldn't do that. Accepting his money negated her principles, made her into someone who would go crying to a benefactor whenever the going got tough. Taking his money made her dependent.

"Think about it," he said. "All of it."

He drew away from her. "Don't leave me, Jonathan."

"Remember? Mrs. Archibald," he said gently. "You have business to transact this afternoon. I'll go to your parents' home and see what mischief Auntie Lou and Adam have gotten into. Meet me there when you're done."

"Jonathan—"

"We'll still have seventy-five percent of the time for us," he promised. He blew her a kiss and went out the door.

Darcy stood at her desk. Intense emotions boiled within her. Confusion. Fear about losing him. Fear about losing herself. Anger. Hurt. More confusion, predominantly confusion. What to do? Who to be?

With the practice of years, she forced the lid over her feelings. Later. She would think about this later. Jonathan was correct. She had a full afternoon of work.

With the sort of revulsion she would experience in touching a worm, she picked up his twenty thousand dollars in cash and carried it to Karen's desk in the outer office. "Please go downstairs to the bank and put this in my deposit box."

"Don't you mean that I should deposit it in your account?"

"No," Darcy said thoughtfully. "Not yet."

Back in her office, she peeled off her suit jacket and rolled up her sleeves. She called Terrence, the investor, who gleefully refused to negotiate. He wanted the Renoir.

She telephoned Mrs. Archibald's son in New York and discovered that he was both devastated by his turn of bad luck and determined to save the painting. "I would have declared bankruptcy," he confessed, "but I couldn't let Mother lose her Renoir."

They'd talked about assets and deficits and projected renewals. Though she was reluctant to arrange a loan to pay on another loan, Darcy spun through her Rollodex of contacts and bankers and Realtors.

The most she could arrange on such short notice was thirty thousand dollars. When she called the son to inform him, he was pleased to tell her that he'd come up with fifty thousand on his own. "Personal loan on my signature," he said.

"Be sure you take care of that person. And relax. I think we've got the situation under control."

All she needed for Mrs. Archibald to keep her

Renoir was twenty thousand dollars. Jonathan's twenty thousand dollars.

Still wanting to keep her emotions at bay, she drove to her parents' house with the car radio playing loud on a classical music station. Unfortunately, her emotional needs were obnoxiously persistent. The violins reminded her of soft candlelight and romance. The horns and tympany sounded like stress and pressure. If a whole orchestra could take such different sounds and themes, melding them into a harmonious whole, why couldn't she accept the variety of her own personality? Be a trumpet one day, and a violin the next.

She parked in the driveway and whisked into the parlor of her parents' home. A loud meeting was in session with Jonathan, her mother, Auntie Lou, and her father.

Jonathan rose to greet her. His gaze reflected her own confusion as he took her hand and led her to a seat.

"About time," her father said. "What we're talking about here is the publicity stuff. That's your bailiwick, Darcy."

"Oh no," Auntie Lou said. "We are discussing the theme for the maiden run. I happen to think there should be balloons. So cheerful, aren't they?"

"And full of hot air," her father muttered. "Louisa, when I said publicity, I meant the theme for the opening. And I think we ought to have a brass band."

"Oh no," Auntie Lou said. "Something elegant."

"Or energetic," Darcy's mother put in. "Aerobics."

"Ladies in tights?" her father questioned. "No, Emma. That's not railroads. We need drums and a Sousa march."

Auntie Lou confronted Jonathan. "And we also need you to be there, Jonathan."

"I'll be there," he agreed. "But I don't want to announce it ahead of time."

Darcy's mother turned to her and asked, "What do you think, dear? Should we have ballet or a big brass band?"

"Or balloons," Auntie Lou added.

Four pairs of eyes focused on Darcy, and the absurdity of the situation struck her. These people were seriously worked up about something as trivial as balloons. All afternoon, she'd been talking with Mrs. Archibald's son, a man who was on the raw edge of disaster, and Mrs. Archibald herself, a woman who was struggling to be brave in the face of a horrendous personal loss.

How could Darcy's family be so eccentric? Crazy dreamers. "It's much too late to be worrying about this."

A cacophony of protest greeted her logic.

"All right." She took a deep breath and said, "I think we should declare the maiden run to be a party for nudists. We can all parade naked through Grand Central Station. Or, better yet, we can rent chicken suits for the entire party. Doesn't that sound like fun?''

"Darcy, please," her Auntie Lou reprimanded.

"What about costumes," Darcy continued. "Maybe we should play dress up in 1900s style clothes. Or in something equally appropriate to the railroads. Like an engineer's suit. And, Poppa, you might decide to illustrate the importance of cattle to railroading. You and Auntie Lou could dress up as Bossy the Cow. Auntie Lou could be the head, and you could be the—"

"Watch it, young lady."

"I like it," Emma said cheerfully.

"1900s costumes," Auntie Lou agreed. "It is elegant."

"No way in blue blazes," Poppa said. "I want a band."

His wife reached over and touched his arm. "Adam, I think it's a wonderful idea." She glanced at the portrait above the mantel. "You could come as Lucky Jim himself."

"I could?" His gaze traveled to the portrait. "I could. There is a resemblance, don't you think?"

"Wait!" Darcy said. "I was joking about costumes. We don't need to create more complications than we already have."

"But it's a charming plan," her mother said. "All in favor?"

She, Poppa, and Auntie Lou raised their hands.

While Darcy glared, Jonathan took a stand with them.

"Next order of business?" he asked.

"Oh, I think that's everything," said Auntie Lou. She rose from her antimaccassared chair with an excited bustle.

Her father marched over to the portrait and stared before swinging back around. "I know where Lucky Jim's old watch chain is hiding. Emma, help me. It's in the attic."

In a flurry, the Conways scattered from the room. Darcy and Jonathan were alone. She stalked to the parlor door and closed it firmly before wheeling around to confront him.

"How could you?" she demanded. "How could you side with them against me?"

"Though you proposed 1900s costumes facetiously, the idea had merit, struck a chord. This wasn't a matter of them or you."

"Yes, it was. Don't you understand, Jonathan. It's always a matter of them versus me. Ever since I was a little girl, they've been telling me not to be so serious, to enjoy life, to show a little *joi de vivre*. They have never accepted who I am."

He leaned back in the huge wingback chair by the fireplace. "Haven't they? And who are you, Darcy?"

"You should certainly know by now."

"Not really. You've told me what you're not. You've insisted that you are not a lady, not a romantic, not a dreamer. Then, who are you?"

The lid she'd placed on her emotions earlier that afternoon would not stay in place. Her control was like a pressure cooker with steam building toward an explosion.

She marched across the room and plopped down in a chair, facing him like a boxer in the ring waiting for the bell to signal round One. "I am a practical, realistic adult female of this time and decade. How dare you suggest that my family knows me better than I know myself."

"Practical and realistic?" He regarded her through steepled fingers. "Yet, this afternoon, you were talking about chucking your business and running away with me."

"A passing fancy," she snapped.

"From a woman who is not a dreamer? Darcy, I believe there is a part of you that really wants to abandon responsibilities and live a carefree life."

"What if there is?" she demanded.

"I want to encourage that. Nothing would give me more pleasure than sweeping you off your beautiful feet."

"You've done that once," she reminded him. "On the slopes at Aspen? Surely you remember, Jonathan. I ended up with a sprained wrist."

"Because you've been hurt, are you afraid to try again?"

"Of course not," she denied quickly, perhaps too quickly. "That wouldn't be practical."

"But you couldn't accept my offer to help out one

of your clients," he pointed out. "How could you accept the easy life that I would willingly, happily give to you?"

"I need more time to figure out my decision."

"What is this decision?"

In her head, the bell for Round One sounded with terrifying clarity and Darcy knew that someone was going to be hurt. "Whether I should run away with you. Or forget you."

She saw the familiar coolness descend over his features. "It's your decision," he said.

Her poise matched his own. "Whether I should stay independent, stay in my own business, my own life. Or give it up and go with you."

"You don't have to give up anything, Darcy."

"Oh no? Well, how can we have a relationship when you're half-way around the world? And how could I run a business if I only check in once every few weeks?"

"You're not being quite accurate. While I've been gone, most of my time has been spent in my home offices in northern California. Or in New York working out the regulations and permits needed for the Twentieth Century. This isn't my normal schedule. I'm usually gone only two days a week."

"So, you'd expect me to relocate my business in northern California."

"That's a possibility."

She shook her head. This decision wasn't about business at all. It was about commitment. Did she really believe in her relationship with Jonathan? Did she trust him enough to join her life with his? "What would happen if you got tired of me?"

"Trust me, that's not likely to occur."

In a frantic burst of energy, her emotions boiled over and Darcy completely lost control.

"Why should I trust you? You haven't proposed marriage, Jonathan. In fact, when I look over these weeks we've spent not seeing each other, not touching each other, you've never even said that you love me. You've offered exactly nothing, no commitment. All you've done is to stand in judgment, like my family, telling me that I'm too stodgy and stable. You've taken advantage of my organizational work to launch your stupid train. You put so much into your dreams, demanding that I share them, but you don't offer a thing in reality. Nothing."

"I'm sorry you feel like that, Darcy."

"So am I. God, so am I." She stood, pulled herself together and lifted her head high. "Goodbye, Jonathan."

TEN

At sunrise, he wakened on a stone bench outside Chicago's Shedd Aquarium. His mouth tasted like bilge water. His limbs, as he stood and stretched, were stiff and sore. He hadn't meant to fall asleep under the city lights and the early springtime moon. But it was morning. Another morning. The third morning since Darcy said goodbye.

Only four more days until his dream of resurrecting the Twentieth Century would be fulfilled. And Jonathan didn't give a damn.

The diffuse morning noise of the busy city surrounded him. Yet when Jonathan Hillcroft, reclusive billionaire, flexed his cramped leg muscles and followed the concrete ramps to the edge of Lake Michigan, he walked alone.

There were no bodyguards, no associates, and no

schedule that he intended to keep. No one in his vast international organization knew where he was. Nor were they likely to find out. In his Levis, sneakers, and black parka, most people wouldn't give him a second glance. His jaw was covered with three days' growth of beard. His sandy hair was disheveled.

Like a hermit, he thought. Finally, he was fulfilling the media stories, and he didn't care. He'd gladly leave the ambition and the stress to someone else.

His back ached from carrying the weight of the world, and he moved stiffly beside the cold, dark waters toward the Gold Coast condominiums. Maybe he should change his name again, maybe start over, go back to being Hogswindler. Those hadn't been such bad times, making deals on a wing and a prayer, living outside acceptable society like a renegade—a pirate whose ship had come in full of treasure.

Could he do it again? Take the risks? Live on the edge?

Probably not, he jeered at himself. Wealth had made him conservative. There was too much to lose from mistakes. Nowadays, he consulted specialists in his research department. No more seat of the pants decisions based on lucky hunches. Jonathan had responsibilities, couldn't take chances. He was a rich man, but dull. And scared.

Too frightened to expose his precious self with Darcy. As Hogswindler, he wouldn't have let her say goodbye. He would have played the odds, taken her into his arms and told her how much he loved her, how he couldn't stop thinking about her, how she dominated his mind and heart.

Loving her was risky, and Jonathan Hillcroft the billionaire hadn't been able to do it. Instead, he hid behind his rigid facade and allowed her to walk out of his life.

Now everything else seemed meaningless.

He climbed into the used car he'd bought for cash at Honest Andy's lot and cruised through the Loop in downtown Chicago. The tall, unnaturally tall, buildings suffocated him. Their glass and steel vistas were too different from home in northern California. Too cold. Too tall. He drove toward less commercial areas and parked outside a school where children had begun to appear on the asphalt playground.

Jonathan closed his eyes and saw himself as a boy, dragging his feet on the way to school, dreading the teacher's disapproval when she caught him daydreaming. Or worse, called on him when he was too shy to answer. School was hell. He preferred to sell oranges on the street corner. Round, succulent fruits that smelled citric and sweet. Once, a boy twice Jonathan's size had tried to steal his oranges and they'd fought. Jonathan had won.

He opened his eyes. A mother was escorting her first grade boy across the street, and she eyed Jonathan suspiciously, like a mother bear guarding her cub. He blinked and saw in his mind the grassy cemetery where his own mother was buried. He had not been able to protect her from a hostile world.

Jonathan started the car engine. The children's shouts and giggles from the playground saddened him. Where were his children? He had no real home, no family to need and depend upon him. Darcy had been right when she lectured about the despair of rich people. There were some things his money could not buy.

He drove aimlessly until he came to the Chicago train yard, one of the largest in the world, miles and miles of tracks. He parked and left the car.

Walking back through his memories, he slogged through a muddy, weed-filled lot until he came to a six-foot tall fence. He laced his fingers through the chain links and stared at the freight trains. An outmoded form of transportation, they bumped lethargically through the yard like sooty, greasy dinosaurs.

The train yard wasn't a pretty scene. Not glamorous or genteel, it was dirty and loud, populated by cold, hard men. At one time, he'd thought those men were gods with the magic power to control those powerful engines. So long ago.

Jonathan stood there for hours. The sun climbed overhead and began its descent. In his mind, he heard the faraway whistle of the trains in the night. And the vibrating rumble along the tracks as they sped on journeys to distant, exotic places.

Jonathan straightened. A realization struck him with ten-ton force. He ran his hand across the rough stubble on his jaw and listened for a moment to the echo in his brain. He didn't want to be alone. For years he'd been guarding his privacy. But he didn't want to be alone anymore. Since childhood, he'd dreamed of a mythical place. But he did not want to live there by himself, to journey there alone.

He knew his journey, the route he wanted to follow. His destination was not a fantastic dream; the place he longed to be was Darcy's real embrace. He could not allow her to slip away from him, to become a faded memory as dim and sad as the filthy train yard that sprawled before him.

He turned his face to the setting sun, waiting until the clouds scudded past and he could feel the warmth of its rays, generating a heat within him. He would not allow the love he felt for Darcy to end with a cold, quiet whimper.

From a telephone booth, he called her office. Her secretary put him right through. "Hello, Darcy."

"Jonathan! Thank God, you're all right."

"I want to see you. Tonight."

"Where are you?" Her voice quivered on a high-pitched tremble. "My God, don't you know what's been going on? Haven't you seen a newspaper?"

"A newspaper?"

"There's a manhunt on for you. APB's all over the country and abroad. The FBI is involved. There was talk of possible kidnapping."

Jonathan slid down the side of the telephone booth and sat on the floor. "How? Why?"

"You didn't show up where you were supposed to be. The last anyone saw of you was at Midway Airfield. As far as I can figure, somebody panicked and contacted the media."

"But it was no big deal. I went to the jet, picked up some clothes, and took a taxi." He paused, remembering his movements of three days ago. "But you're right. I didn't tell anyone."

"I've been so frightened. If anything had happened to you, I don't know what I would have done."

"I'm all right. And I want to see you."

"I want to see you, too." She paused. "And I'm not the only one. Your disappearance has been big news, sensational headline news. Worse, there have been rumbles through the financial community, some unloading of stock. You're going to have to hold a press conference, Jonathan."

With a shudder, he imagined what his disappearance could do to his worldwide empire. Too many people depended upon his decisions for the final word.

But why this panic? This search? Though he didn't make a practice of disappearing once a week, he had taken off before on unscheduled vacations. Who among his staff would be stupid enough to release that information to the press?

"Darcy?" Jonathan remembered his priorities. He would have to deal with this situation, but the first order of business was Darcy. "I won't do anything until I see you."

"You can't do that! The whole world is waiting for news about you."

"Then the whole damn world will have to wait. You're more important. The way I feel about you is more important than headlines and rumors and financial rumbles." His pulse hammered in his wrist. "I love you, Darcy."

There was a moment of silence on the telephone before she replied. "I love you, too."

"Meet me at the . . ." he stopped himself. If all these people were looking for him, her telephone might very well be bugged. ". . . meet me at the place where my dreams are becoming reality."

"What? Jonathan, I don't want to play James Bond."

"Do you understand where I mean? A *limited* number of people would understand."

"I know where you mean."

"Come alone, Darcy. I want to see you alone." He hung up the telephone.

Darcy's hand trembled on the telephone receiver. Had she really spoken to him? Dizzy with relief, she folded her arms on her desk and laid her head down. Thank God he was safe! During the past three days, Jonathan's top aides had been in constant touch with Darcy and her family. There had been nonstop questions and nonstop fears. And her own private hell.

She couldn't forget the last contact she'd had with him—when she flounced out of the parlor like a spoiled child who wouldn't play unless she got everything her way. She'd recalled that scene a million times in her mind, torturing herself with guilt.

She raised her head from the desk. Jonathan was all right. He'd called her. He'd said that he loved her. And he wanted to see her. Alone.

Alone? This might be complicated. For the past three days, she had been one of the major focus points for the search. His bodyguards and aides and an aggressive FBI agent had been harrassing her for information. Darcy paused. Would it be illegal to meet him without telling anyone? Harboring a fugitive? She had never in her life intentionally disobeyed authority, never walked on the grass when a sign said not to. She never even removed the tags on foam pillows.

This was different. Jonathan needed her, and she would manage to meet him alone. She called her secretary into her office and said, "You know that was Jonathan on the telephone, don't you?"

Karen Parelli bit off a fingernail and nodded. These days of intense pressure had been hard on her, too.

"I'm going to meet him," Darcy said. "Alone."

"Fat chance. Two of Jonathan's aides are in the outer office right this minute. Reading the Dow Jones and wringing their hands. They want to drive you home."

"I'll tell them I have an appointment."

"Good luck, boss lady." Karen offered a smile. "Oh, while you were on the phone with you-know-who, Mrs. Archibald called to thank you for saving her Renoir."

Darcy nodded. Instead of using Jonathan's money, she'd cleaned out her personal savings to meet the deadline payment. It hadn't been the most efficient solution, but it was the only one she could come up with under pressure. "Call her back, tell her I'll be in touch, and remind her about the maiden run of the Twentieth Century."

"Done."

Darcy straightened the collar of her black serge suit, picked up her coat, and concentrated on keeping her hands from shaking. "Do I look like someone going on an appointment?"

"You might want to take your briefcase."

"Oh, right. Briefcase."

Darcy grabbed the suede briefcase, pasted a casual smile on her face and breezed past the two men lurking in her outer office. "No time to talk. Business, business."

"Wait, Ms. Conway."

"No time to talk. Big time deal. Later."

She pushed through the door to her office, stepped into the elevator and gritted her teeth. Did they believe her?

Daylight in the parking lot was beginning to fade when she clenched her left hand around the steering wheel of her BMW and turned the ignition key. What would she do if someone followed her? A maneuver like the one Jonathan used in Aspen? She cruised through the parking lot of the shopping center on the opposite side of the boulevard, watching in her rearview mirror. After several double-backs, she decided that she was not being pursued. Still, she whipped through the rear loading area behind the center and took off through the side streets.

Jonathan had referred to the place where his dream was kept, his limited dream. Obviously, he meant the warehouse where the Twentieth Century Limited was being renovated.

Keeping her speed to a steady, law-abiding pace was almost impossible; she was so anxious to see him. When she parked outside the warehouse, it was after quitting time and there were no other cars in the lot. Had she misunderstood Jonathan's instructions? Where was he?

She checked her wristwatch. Fourteen minutes late. She dashed from the car and into the small side door of the warehouse. It was unlocked.

In contrast to the beat-up barn where they'd first seen Engine 5252, this warehouse was clean and well-tended. Though Darcy had only been there once, a couple of weeks ago, she knew from her father's reports that the renovation work was progressing nicely. But still she was shocked by the sight that greeted her.

Engine 5252 had been refitted, cleaned, and polished. It was beautiful. The black steel gleamed, emanating the incredible potential of powerful speed. Every rivet sparkled. The huge wheels had been stripped of rust, and the spokes painted an enameled red like the repaired cowcatcher on the front. A large, shiny brass bell sat on a worktable, waiting to be hung from the front of the engine.

It was Jonathan's dream come true. "Jonathan," she whispered. "Where are you?"

She stood very still and listened to the creaks and moans from the rafters of the warehouse. No human sound reached her ears. Where was he? What if it wasn't Jonathan on the telephone? Maybe this was a hoax. Maybe he'd been kidnapped after all.

A dark figure emerged from the rear of Engine 5252. He came toward her with long, athletic strides.

"Jonathan!" she cried. Her voice echoed in the cool warehouse.

They ran toward each other and met, clinging together in the shadow of his dream engine. Their entwined shape reflected in the polished brass of the bell. Darcy sobbed with relief. She clutched him to her, willing him to never leave again, and wept on his shoulder.

"It's all right," he murmured softly. "I'm sorry, Darcy."

"You should be." Her breath heaved in spasms. "Oh God, Jonathan, I thought I'd never see you again."

"I'm here."

He held her until the unleashed storm of her emotions subsided to small, hiccuping gasps. Then he took her by the shoulders, stroked her forehead and wiped a streaked tear from her cheek. "As you can see, I'm all right. As Mark Twain once said, 'Reports of my death have been greatly exaggerated.' "

She beheld his face, his handsome Adonis face, as if it were the first time she'd really seen him. Never before had she felt such intense fulfillment. He was safe.

"Jonathan, I never meant to hurt you."

"I know."

She allowed a deep sigh to escape her lips. It felt like the first time she'd really breathed in three days. "Have you read the newspapers?"

He nodded, his expression was serious. "This situation is going to take some strategic planning to untangle. But I want to talk to you first."

"Why? Jonathan, the FBI has been involved. And the police. I might be doing something illegal by coming here to see you."

"You? A felon?" He laughed. "Don't worry, Darcy. I haven't done anything remotely criminal. Unless there's a law against self-pity."

"There probably should be," she said, glad to hear his laughter. "Why did you disappear?"

"I needed time to think, to evaluate my life."

"I can tell you this, everyone else thinks you're pretty important. I've never seen so many concerned, hysterical people."

"Yes, indeed. Concerned about who would sign their paychecks on Friday. That was one of my great self-discoveries, Darcy. About my business. I kept remembering how it used to be when I was young and broke and not afraid to take chances. Preserving the Hillcroft empire has made me too conservative, always worrying about how I can take care of everything for everyone. Well, it's time I delegate more authority, allow them to test their own wings, take responsibility for themselves."

"What else did you think about?"

"The most important facets of life: My dreams. And my love."

She looked at the massive, beautiful locomotive. "Your dream is doing very well. It's fantastic."

"And my love is in my arms." He hugged her close to him. "Never leave me again, Darcy."

Her smile was weak, barely crinkling the corners of her eyes. She was tired. The release of her tension had left her limp. Not to mention that the sleep she'd gotten during the last few days could be counted in minutes, not hours. Still, his words piqued her temper. "I wasn't the one who left."

"You said goodbye."

"But I didn't vanish from the face of the planet. I've had a chance to do some thinking, too."

"About love?"

She broke away from him and went to the worktable, trailing her fingertips over the brass bell. Love should be such a simple emotion, following a natural sequence of love, then marriage and a family. Yet, she saw nothing but complications in her future.

Throughout the ordeal of his disappearance, she'd been made aware of how important he was—internationally important. Entire corporations depended on him. He was a world figure.

In the idealized world of love, she could insist that he curtail his travels and pay more attention to her. In reality, such demands were short-sighted and insignificant compared to his other responsibilities.

"About my naivety," she said. "Maybe because I've spent my life among people who were wealthy, I didn't realize how special you are, how important. Hemingway was right when he said, 'The very rich are different from you and me.' "

" 'Yes,' " Jonathan completed the quote, " 'they have more money.' "

She grinned. "Darn all those books in your library. I can never sneak past you with a quote, can I?"

"I'm not so sharp on the Far East prophets," he said.

"Ah so, how about this." She hoisted herself onto the worktable and tried to look inscrutable. "Confucius say: Man with big bucks has no time for woman with big mouth."

"You made that up, and it's not true on either count. I have time for you. You are all I have time for. And you don't have a big mouth.'' In response to her disbelieving chuckle, he added, ''Your mouth is in perfect proportion to the rest of your lovely face.''

''What are you going to do about the newspapers?''

''Now's not the time to deal with that, not when there is something much more important. I still need to talk with you.''

The thoroughness of his attention unnerved her. Though it was flattering to believe that she took precedence over world affairs, she was skeptical.

''Let me tell you a story,'' he said. ''A long time ago, I met an old man who was once an engineer on the railroad. Engineering had been his lifelong dream and he was happy in his work. But he quit. His wife was ill, dying. He quit his dream to be with her until the end when he laid her to rest.''

She fidgeted but remained sitting on the worktable, her feet dangling in air. ''This is a sad story, Jonathan.''

''Not at all. Because this old man was content. Though he couldn't find another job and his only money came from gathering aluminum cans for redemption, he considered himself one of the luckiest men on earth. He'd fulfilled a dream. And he had known true love. Most people don't experience either. He'd had both.''

He stood before her. ''I want both, Darcy. You are my own true love, my once in a lifetime love. I want for us to be together forever—''

"Wait, Jonathan." She placed her finger on his lips. "I can't make a decision."

"You can, Darcy. Trust your feelings. You know it's right for us to be together. We'll work out the details."

"No. I'm afraid."

"Of being hurt? Darcy, I will never hurt you."

"It's not you." She spoke slowly and carefully. "For half my life, I thought I was afraid of being hurt. By people like Thomas O'Bannion. And by my family, of course. I've built walls and sheltered myself behind them, refused to think about commitments . . ."

"And to dream?"

"Oh yes, Jonathan. I've been so afraid my dreams wouldn't come true, that there was a horrible nightmare lurking in every bright fantasy."

" 'Be careful what you dream,' " he quoted. " 'Because you just might get it.' "

"Yes, and when you disappeared, I discovered another fear. A fear as big as the Twentieth Century Limited. I'm more afraid of hurting someone else. Of hurting you, Jonathan. Please don't ask me for a commitment. I can't answer you until I understand this fear. I love you. Can that be enough for now?"

"Yes." He glided his hands around her shoulders. "For now."

He pulled her from her perch on the workbench,

and they embraced, impelled by a poignant attraction. Their lips met for a brief kiss, the merest tasting
of commitment. Then, they separated.

"Please, Jonathan, you have to do something
about being missing. I've been at the eye of this
hurricane search for you, and it's cruel to prolong
it."

"All right." He led her across the warehouse to
a small glassed-in office with a telephone. "I'll call
my aides and issue a brief press release."

"That's a start, but you know that's not enough.
A statement to the press could look like a cover-up."

"Are you saying that I have to face the music?
Hold a press conference to prove to everyone that I
have all my limbs and my mental faculties intact?"

"It might be easier than living with the rumors."

She well understood his reluctance to step into the
harsh glare of the spotlight. His reaction mirrored
her own. After only three days of constant telephone
calls and visits from Jonathan's staff, she'd been
ready to bury her head in the sand like an ostrich.
Still, she reminded him, "You have responsibilities."

"But I also have a responsibility to myself. And
to you. Would the world crumble if we sailed off
together to a deserted island?" He picked up the
telephone on the desk in the office and mused on the
possibility. "I could be a coconut picker. And you
would look great in a sarong."

"Life isn't that simple."

"Not my life or yours, anyway."

While he used the telephone to dial his private number, she sank into the padded chair behind the desk in the small office, kicked off her shoes and stretched her feet out on the desk. Until she got comfortable, Darcy didn't realize how exhausted and tense she had been. Nor how relieved she now felt, knowing Jonathan was safe and secure. And that he loved her. His one true love.

She listened as he made explanations and gave orders: "Issue a statement to the effect that I took an unscheduled vacation to an unspecified location. I happened to be out of touch. And emphasize that at no time was I in any physical danger."

That sounded quite plausible, she thought. With a lazy finger, she traced a circle on her knee, then a looping figure eight. The symbol for eternity. An eternity with him. Forever didn't seem long enough.

"Schedule a press conference in Chicago at noon tomorrow," he instructed. "And one more thing. Do you have any idea who leaked this story to the press?"

She saw him stiffen. Then he laughed, long and loud. The rest of the conversation was interspersed with disbelieving comments and more laughter.

When he hung up the telephone, his grey eyes sparkled and his lips were split in a wide grin. "An interesting development, Darcy. My staff has traced the leak."

Darcy had a horrible premonition. "Oh? And who was the idiot that called the press."

"Oh, it wasn't just a call to the press. Something like that might have been logged under a crank contact and dismissed. No, indeed. This leak contacted all three major network news stations, eleven newspapers, and a national tabloid. It was very thorough. And very clever. The various branches of the media contacted each other, and the rumor verified itself."

"Why are you laughing?" Darcy asked.

"Because the individual who arranged this media blitz was none other than your father, Adam Conway."

"Oh my God." She buried her face in her hands. How could her father have done such a thing? Didn't he realize the repercussions?

"Actually, Darcy, this is less your fault than anyone else's. You've been telling me since the day we met that your family is eccentric, prone to bizarre behavior. And I've dismissed your warnings. I didn't think they could cause any harm." He tucked a stray hair behind her ear and placed a light kiss on her ivory cheek. "Now, isn't there something you'd like to say to me?"

"I-told-you-so."

"Yes, you did. I'm going to have to learn to pay more attention."

He tenderly suited the action to the word. For a scant quarter of an hour, Jonathan and Darcy shared the sweet relief of caresses and warm gentle words. Then, his staff swarmed the warehouse.

After promising to meet him at the hotel in the morning, Darcy boarded her BMW and set a determined course for her parents' house.

ELEVEN

Adam Conway didn't even have the good sense to appear contrite. He leaned back in his office chair, puffing one of his foul-smelling cigars and listened to Darcy lambaste him up one side and down the other. "You caused an international panic! Of all the irresponsible, wild-eyed ideas you've ever had, this is the worst. Why, Poppa?"

"I wanted to get a hold of Johnny and I couldn't."

"So you called eleven newspapers and three television networks?"

"I figured that if anybody could find him, they could."

Darcy was sputtering helplessly when her leotard-clad mother slipped into the room and took a position behind her husband. She braced her hand on the back of his chair and did a quick knee bend.

"There's something you should understand," Emma said. "Your father might have been very wrong in his solution, but his motivation was good."

"What motivation?" Darcy stormed. "Did he want to talk with Jonathan about the color of placemats in the Twentieth Century?"

"You were the motivation," her mother said.

"Me? What on God's green earth does this have to do with me?"

"He was worried about you, dear. It was rather apparent that you and Jonathan had a tiff, and your father did not want to see your relationship come to an end."

"I like Johnny," Adam said gruffly. "I'd like him for a son-in-law, and I couldn't sit by while he took off to leave you high and dry."

"Poppa, it's my life, my decisions. Especially about Jonathan. You can't run it for me."

"I know." He puffed his thick cigar. "But that doesn't stop me from wanting to protect my little girl."

"We want what's best for you," her mother said. "We want you to be healthy and happy."

Her father cleared his throat. The corners of his mouth pulled down in a fierce scowl. "We love you, Darcy."

Darcy stood for a moment, staring at these two people who had brought her into the world. Over the twenty-eight years of her life, they had nursed her through illness and consoled her and teased her and praised her and argued with her. And loved her. Her parents might be world-class eccentrics, but Darcy knew their hearts were in the right place.

Hands on hips, Darcy stood before her father. "Poppa, you're an interfering, manipulative monster. Half the time, you drive me crazy. Your ideas about life and relationships are dated by nearly one hundred years." She reached down, took the cigar from his lips and stuffed it in the ashtray. "And I love you very much."

She wrapped him in a big hug. "Don't you ever pull anything like this again."

"You know better than that," her mother said. "I've been warning him for the past forty-two years."

"I know, Mama. He's impossible, isn't he?"

"Hush up, you two," he said. "I won't have you womenfolk talking about me as if I weren't sitting here."

"Fine." Darcy hooked her arm through Emma's. "We'll go talk about you in the parlor."

Darcy and her mother were only halfway down the hall when Adam marched out of his study and placed himself between them, curling one arm around his wife and the other around his daughter. "Women! You can't live with them, and you can't live without them."

"About time you realized that," Emma said. "And I think now might be an appropriate time to discuss your nasty, very unhealthy tobacco habit."

After warm discussions and viewing the costumes her mother and Auntie Lou intended to wear on the maiden run, Darcy spent the night in her old bedroom, enjoying the memories. When she woke there was a smile on her lips. Though she couldn't recall her dreams, the warm sense of pleasure convinced her that they must have been about Jonathan.

In the morning, she swung past her apartment and dressed carefully in a conservative beige linen suit. She stopped at the bank to retrieve Jonathan's twenty-thousand dollars from her safe deposit box, intending to proudly inform him that her negotiations regarding Mrs. Archibald had been accomplished successfully. Then she was on her way to the stylish Black Angus hotel in downtown Chicago.

Darcy knew the protocol for a press conference. Several of her chums from boarding school had married politicians or had run for office themselves, and Darcy had been involved in their fund-raising efforts. Also, the Conway family was on the "A" list for political luncheons, teas, and benefits.

At the hotel, she showed identification to two sets of bodyguards and entered the penthouse suite where Jonathan had arranged to meet her. The press conference was scheduled in half an hour. Though Darcy knew what to expect, she wasn't prepared for the intense excitement that buzzed among Jonathan's aides. Nor for the deference paid to her.

It seemed that Jonathan's staff was utterly delighted that he had finally acknowledged the need for contact with the press. And they supposed that she had something to do with his decision. Their attentions were nearly fawning as she was ushered to a comfortable seat, supplied with lemonade and generally fussed over.

Irritably, she was beginning to feel like a royal consort. The crown prince's mistress.

Jonathan himself barely had time to greet her before an energetic man named Randy, the head of Jonathan's promotion department, led him to a make-up mirror.

Jonathan balked. "Absolutely not. I will not be painted and powdered like a movie star."

"There will be photographs taken," Randy advised. "The lighting from mini-cams tends to wash out your complexion. Please, Jonathan, I'm sure you don't want to appear sick."

"I want to appear as myself," Jonathan said.

Randy appealed to Darcy, "Ms. Conway? Perhaps you could use your influence with Mr. Hillcroft?"

"Perhaps I could," she drawled. "But I happen to agree with him. And I think he looks just fine."

"Thank you."

Before more interruptions could ensue, Jonathan took Darcy by the hand and dragged her through a door which he closed and locked.

"Jonathan, this is the bathroom."

"Yep, it is."

"Not exactly a class move, locking me in the bathroom with you. Somehow, I expected more from an important billionaire.''

''In case you hadn't noticed, I'm not your usual billionaire. And this is the only place I can find peace and quiet. Wearing make-up, for pity's sake. Priming like a showgirl.''

''You seem to have made your staff quite happy.''

''They've been advising me to hold press conferences for years. The need for high visibility, they call it.''

''And what do you call it?''

''A royal pain in the ankle.''

He rested his hands on the countertop and squinted into the wall of bright mirrors. ''Only fifteen minutes to go. Want to take a shower while we're waiting?''

''With twenty people standing outside the door? No thank you, I'm not into voyeurism.''

''If we were married,'' he said, ''would it make a difference?''

''Even if we were . . .'' She couldn't quite bring herself to say the word. ''I would not take a shower with you while your business associates hovered outside the door. Nor would I engage in similar activities, such as mud wrestling.''

''And you call me old-fashioned,'' he teased. ''So, Darcy, have you given any more thought to your decision?''

''Not yet.'' She stood next to him, gazing into the looking glass. It was almost as if there were four people in the bathroom instead of two. Darcy and

Jonathan and their alter egos. She pointed a finger at the glassy surface and traced the line of his jaw. "It's complicated, isn't it?"

"Not at all." His voice echoed slightly against the white tile walls. "I want you with me all the time. I want to wake up each morning and see that beautiful face beside me. And I want children, Darcy. Children with your black hair and blue eyes."

"And your dreams?"

"You are my dream. I've always dreamed of a woman like you. A lady."

A shiver ran through her as she studied their reflection. Was that the woman he really wanted? Darcy in the looking glass, a dreamlike image. Did he really want to deal with all her flesh and blood flaws?

She turned away from the mirror. "I don't want to disappoint you. You've got to be very sure that you want me, the Darcy Conway who has a temper and demands her independence and is afraid of hurting and being hurt."

"Of course." He still regarded her profile in the mirror. "I want you."

She touched his cheek and turned his gaze toward her. "Me, Jonathan. Imperfect me. Not the lady who you think I am."

"You, Darcy Conway. Warts and all."

He took her hand in his, and she felt a shuddering in his fingers. His flesh was icy cold. "Are you ill?"

"Not exactly. I have a fairly warty confession to

make about myself." He cleared his throat. "I'm shy."

"Like the stories in the newspapers?"

"Not that bad. I'm not pathological," he said defensively. "But when it comes to standing up in front of people and talking, I'm scared as a rabbit. That was one of the reasons I did poorly in school. I hated class participation. I would sit there, hiding behind a book and the teacher would call on me and—"

"And you would freeze," she said.

Her focus on Jonathan clarified, and she understood his reputation for reclusiveness in a completely different light. His perfectly rational desire for privacy was only half the picture. Shyness was the other half.

She remembered the first time they shook hands, how aloof he had seemed. At the beginning of the meeting with her family, his features had been immobile. When they were chased by the reporter, Benowski, he was colder than a blizzard in Aspen. He'd constantly refused press attention for the Twentieth Century Limited.

In this context, it made sense to her. Jonathan Hillcroft was shy. Every time he revealed a tiny piece of himself, it required painfully chipping away at a wall of ice.

She gave him a sad smile and said, "My monstrous father with his inappropriate phone calls put you in this position. I feel so guilty."

"You're not to blame, remember? You told me so."

"Telling is different than experiencing. No one can really understand the Conway eccentricity until they've lived with it. And that's no guarantee. I've lived with it all my life, and I still can't fully explain it."

"This isn't Adam's fault," he said. "This press conference is overdue. And I know, rationally and logically, that my promotional people are right. I need to counteract the image of weird hermit Hillcroft, to place myself at the helm, to grin and bear it."

A hesitant tapping came at the bathroom door, and Darcy heard an apologetic, muffled voice warning, "Jonathan? It's time to go? Are you ready?"

She asked, "Can I help you get past the shyness?"

"You could stand next to me with a bucket of water and douse me if I turn to stone."

"Would it help if I stood beside you?"

"I can't ask that of you, Darcy." He gazed back at her mirror image. "There have been rumors about you and me. References to our relationship."

"Like what?"

"That you're my mistress, my lover, my mysterious sex kitten. You're too much of a lady to be subjected to sordid accusations."

"I'm not a painted china doll, Jonathan. And maybe this will prove it to you. This might sound as corny as a country western song, but I will stand by my man. If it will help for me to be there, I will be.''

His grey-eyed gaze was eloquent with a vulnerability that touched her deeply. ''Thank you.''

The tapping at the door had accelerated to a loud, hammering. ''Jonathan! You're all right, aren't you?''

She winked at him. ''It's show time.''

''Good. Let's get it over with.''

Darcy and Jonathan entered the well-filled ballroom of the Black Angus in the center of a phalanx of bodyguards and aides who led them to a podium supplied with a jungle of microphones.

After the flashbulbs had flashed and Jonathan raised his hand for quiet, she took a position to his left, quiet as a proper mouse but there if he needed her. For a shy person, this situation must be like a nightmare come true. There were over forty reporters and photographers as well as three mini-cam crews from the television networks. Their lights aimed at the podium and flared to a blinding glare.

Jonathan's jaw was set at a stubborn angle, and his attitude was so chill that she half-expected the microphones on the podium to frost over as he read a prepared statement: ''I regret the confusion caused by my unexplained absence. It resulted from a missed communication between myself and my staff when I took an unscheduled vacation. I wish to state very clearly that I was not kidnapped. There were no threats on my life. I was in no danger. I appreciate the concern of the world press, and I apologize for the inconvenience.''

''Where were you?'' came a shout from the front row.

''I spent most of my time right here in the Chicago area.''

''Isn't it true, Mr. Hillcroft, that you were conducting secret negotiations in the Middle East?''

''No, not true. And I wish to point out that if I had been aware of this commotion, I would have responded immediately.''

''Mr. Hillcroft? Are you building a supersonic railway system that would link the coasts?''

''No, again. I am, however, involved in a railroad project. The resurrection of the old Twentieth Century Limited which will run an express route between New York City and Chicago. The first trip is scheduled for April first. In three days. And we hope to open the train to the public by June fifteenth.''

Several other questions bounced between the media and Jonathan. Was he founding a new nation in South Africa? Had he bought the state of Arizona? Who really kidnapped him and was the ransom in excess of $5.6 million dollars?

Darcy recognized one of the reporters as Benowski, the man who'd followed them in Aspen. His question sounded more loudly than the others. ''What is your relationship with Miss Conway?''

''Very private.''

He turned to a different reporter, but Benowski

persisted, "Haven't you donated heavily to Ms. Conway's business?"

"No, I have not," Jonathan stated uncomfortably. "Are there any other questions?"

"What about the Archibald affair?" Benowski called out. "I have information that links your name with hers, and again a considerable sum of money. Are you involved with her, too?"

"Mrs. Archibald is near seventy years old," Jonathan said.

While the reporters laughed at Benowski's mistake, Darcy felt a sharp awareness slash through her like a knife. She remembered the fifty thousand dollars that Mrs. Archibald's son had suddenly been able to raise though he was destitute. She knew, as sure as she was standing there, that the money had come from Jonathan.

Still, Benowski shouted, "When are you going to make an honest woman of Ms. Conway?"

Jonathan fixed the reporter with a cold steel gaze. "She is the most honest individual I've ever met."

Despite the continuing clamor, Jonathan raised his hand and waved. "Thank you all for coming. That will be all."

His cluster of bodyguards and aides closed around them, neatly whisking them through the kitchen and out of the room.

At the door to the penthouse suite, Jonathan whipped around and faced his attentive staff. "Thank you all very much. I'll be at the offices tomorrow morning. Right now, I would like a few moments of privacy with Ms. Conway.''

After quick congratulations, the aides and department heads dispersed, leaving only one bodyguard posted outside the suite.

Jonathan closed the door and locked it. ''Publicity is hell,'' he said.

''You did very well.''

''I'm just damn glad it's over.''

When he reached for her, she moved away. ''What did Benowski mean when he said you'd donated money to my business?''

''He meant to be rude, and he succeeded.''

''What about his reference to Mrs. Archibald? You were the mysterious source who came to her son's aid, weren't you?''

He nodded. ''I guess I should have told you.''

''Oh no, you were right not to mention this. Because I would never have accepted. I'm furious, Jonathan. I thought I'd made it crystal clear that I can handle my own business.''

She walked stiff-legged across the ornately furnished living room of the hotel penthouse suite and sank onto an antique loveseat upholstered in chocolate brown velvet. Formerly, the suite had been overpopulated with Jonathan's staff and she hadn't noticed the exquisite old-fashioned detailing. There was a coldness and formality about it that suited her mood.

''Is this an indication of what our life together would be?'' she asked. ''You would allow me to pretend I was in business for myself, but if I ever got into trouble, you'd bail me out?''

He came toward her. ''You know that's not what I want. Let's not play games.''

''And you're a fine one to talk about gamesmanship. You went behind my back. You let me think that I managed to work out a solution to an impossible problem.''

''I know part of your solution, Darcy. I know you put up twenty thousand of your own money. And that puts you in the same class as me.''

''Really? And what class is that?''

''Being a person who's not afraid to put their money to good use. To help someone who needs helping. Even if it's illogical.''

''But it was my business. My decision.''

''Why? When I called Mrs. Archibald's son, I agreed with your opinion. He's a sincere, dedicated young man who happened to fall on some bad times with his business. I know what he's going through. I've been there, Darcy.''

''Oh, please. Don't give me a lecture on how hard you've struggled with your business. I've struggled, too.''

He was taken aback. ''I don't think of you in that way.''

''I know you don't.''

She felt her fears materializing, creating an invisible wall between them, a wall so thick and wide that it could not be penetrated. It was painfully obvious;

he didn't accept her as she really was. His vision was clouded by dream images of a lady, and Darcy knew she would always disappoint him with her reality, always hurt him by not being what he expected.

"From the first time we met," she said, calmly, "you've been trying to second-guess me. And mostly, your judgments have been incorrect because I don't fit the dream you have of me."

"I want to share my dreams with you."

"And what if my reality doesn't fit?"

"I will adjust," he promised.

She wanted so much to believe that. Yet, how could she? She'd learned over and over again what a massively important and powerful man he was. One of the richest men in the world. He could have anything and everything he wanted. How soon would he tire of her small shows of independence? He needed a devoted woman like her mother. Or a lovely woman who wanted to be spoiled with his lavish attentions, like her cousin Paula. It wasn't just her career that got in the way, Darcy decided, it was her. Her self. She didn't fit into his world. Didn't fit into his dreams.

She clicked open her purse, removed the thick envelope containing his twenty thousand dollars and placed it on an oak coffee table. "I can't accept this. And I will find a way to pay back your other investment."

"I love you, Darcy. I love your strength and your stubborn ways. I love who you are."

That was exactly why she needed time to figure this out. His love. She didn't want to spend her life feeling guilty for not being what he wanted. "You know, Jonathan, this would have been easier if we'd met long ago. We could have built our dream castles together."

"It's not too late."

She glanced up at him and smiled. "You've always wanted to go backward in time. And maybe you can. Maybe you can create that reality. But, I don't think I can."

"Will you try?"

"You'll have my answer within the week."

"I won't accept that, Darcy."

He paced away from her. His already intense feelings rose in a turmoil, repeating the echo of self-discovery: he did not want to be alone.

He needed to act, to convince her. Why was this so hard? Sometimes he and Darcy seemed to work against each other like pistons driven by steam. And yet, there was the promise of incredible force if they could harness their power.

"The new Twentieth Century Limited takes its maiden run in three days," he said. "It's very important to me that you be there."

"That's exactly why I need a week. The train is your dream, Jonathan, not mine."

"Why can't it be *our* dream? Yours and mine. If we can't share our dreams, how can we hope to build anything? Make a commitment to me, Darcy. Share with me. Together, we could ride to the stars.''

"What about all the details in between? The logistics of this commitment. Where would we live? How will we find time to be together? What about my business?''

"I trust that we can work out the details.'' He held out his hand to her. "But I can see that you need time to think. And, frankly, I'm not going to beg you. Take time for your decision.''

"A week?''

"That will be too late.''

When she rose to her feet and placed her fingertips in his hand, he clasped lightly. Very formally, he escorted her to the door of the penthouse suite and opened it. "Goodbye, Darcy Conway. I will see you in three days at the maiden run of the Twentieth Century Limited.''

He closed the door behind her.

_____ TWELVE _____

On a platform at Chicago's Grand Central Station, Engine 5252, renovated as a diesel locomotive, posed majestically beneath heavy garlands of roses. In the midst of the hoopla, she was ready for her maiden journey.

It was early evening, after the suburban commuters had already departed on their more mundane trains, and the Twentieth Century was placed at the furthest track from regular railroad business. The gleaming engine stood at the head of a six-car train with four Pullmans, a dining car, and a charming early 1900s parlor.

A five-man brass band, directed by Adam Conway, serenaded the imminent departure time, and the atmosphere of excitement played itself to a frenzied pitch.

Despite late notice, most of the passengers, including press, had chosen to dress in early 1900s garb. The ladies' huge feathered hats bobbed festively while gentlemen dusted their spats and consulted ornate gold pocketwatches.

From the top of the stairs overlooking the platform, Darcy watched the festivities with a mixture of pride and sadness. The recreation of the Twentieth Century Limited was a marvelous spectacle, Jonathan's dream come true. Yet, she was not a part of it.

She had not contacted him during the past three days, and she feared that with each moment passing she was growing further and further away from him. Ultimately, the train would chug away from the station and they would be forever beyond each other's grasp.

Though her heart urged her to descend the stair to the platform, her fears held her back. If she took this step, the commitment was sealed. Both she and Jonathan understood that. If she stayed away, their relationship was over.

Though she gripped the handrail of the bannister with tense, whitened knuckles, she couldn't help smiling as she watched Paula make her grand entrance to the platform. Darcy's blonde, beautiful cousin was glamorous in a lacey white dress and a feather-trimmed hat that must have been three feet in diameter. Clinging to Paula's arm was an Aspen hunk who had chosen to dress as a buckskinned mountaineer.

Darcy saw her mother athletically pumping hands and working the crowd. Emma wore a delicate maroon dress that skimmed her slender torso attractively. Auntie Lou, dripping with furs, bustled about in a plain, floor-length black taffeta gown. Even Darcy's secretary, Karen, had dressed in a long, green suit appropriate to the period.

The men were not so resplendent. Their suits were black or grey or pinstriped, some with brocaded vests. About half the men wore bowler hats and the other half skimmers. Most of them, like Poppa, were swaggering, smoking fat cigars.

She didn't see Jonathan.

Perhaps, he was already on the train.

A few people had already boarded, but the majority stayed on the platform, being served cocktails by white-jacketed porters.

Darcy gathered up her black handbag and pulled her wrap more tightly around her shoulders. Perhaps, she should leave now, wave a silent farewell and disappear through Grand Central Station to the bustling streets of the city where cars and buses followed rational routes to specific destinations. That was her world, the place where she had made a safe niche for herself, a flat horizon without unwanted confusion and surprises.

Shouts of cheerful greeting resounded from the throne gathered below her, like the tiny metal figures she arranged for Jonathan's model train, and she stayed to watch another dramatic entrance. A very old-fashioned looking woman in a wheelchair appeared on the platform. Darcy could see wisps of her upswept white hair beneath a conservative black hat. It was Mrs. Archibald.

The tall, handsome man pushing the wheelchair was Jonathan.

He'd dressed in black suit with bowler hat, exactly like the figure who stood beside his model of the Twentieth Century.

Darcy knew her place was beside him.

Slowly, she descended to the platform.

The crowd seemed to part before her, and she could see only Jonathan, a man from a more genteel era, the man of her dreams.

When he beheld her, she recognized the love beaming from his grey-eyed gaze because it matched her own, mesmerized stare. It was as if they were meeting for the first time, and she recalled her very first words to him: "Mr. Hillcroft? I'm Darcy Conway."

She extended her hand. Instead of a handshake, he kissed her fingertips and she felt the thrill down to her toes. "Haven't we met before?"

"Yes," she whispered. "In my dreams."

She took his arm, completing a destined picture. Darcy had dressed in a high-necked, white blouse, floor-length black skirt, and wide-brimmed black hat with dark roses at the crown—a precise copy of the tiny enamelled figure of the 1902 suffragette.

While she and Jonathan politely acted the parts of host and hostess for this historic ride, Darcy felt a grand sense of fulfillment. Her face was flushed bright red, and she could feel her blue eyes shining with happy, unshed tears. Her smile came from deep within her.

Jonathan was marvelous. His deep voice rumbled in pleased welcome, putting every passenger at ease, even being gallant with the press. At the same time, he made Darcy feel like the only woman in the world.

Her father marched up to them. "About time, Darcy."

"You look just like Lucky Jim," she said.

"But there is a difference, my dear." He tapped the front of his gold brocaded vest. "In here."

Her mother joined them, linking arm with Adam. "Thank God."

Adam Conway made a great show of pulling his gold watch from his pocket and consulting it. "If we want to stay on schedule, we'd best be going, Jonathan."

"You're right."

Tearing his gaze away form Darcy, Jonathan waved to the blue-suited conductor who cupped his hands around his mouth and began the chant. "All aboard. Ladies and gentlemen, the Twentieth Century Limited will be departing in five minutes. All aboard.''

The brass bell affixed to Engine 5252 began to clang.

In a few minutes, the parlor car was full with the white-jacketed bartender working lickety-split to fill orders and other porters circulating with drinks and canapes.

Darcy edged closer to Jonathan. "Might need a second parlor," she said.

"Come with me." He led her through a private exit behind the bartender, to the rear of the train.

They stood together on a rear platform made of steel. A black steel bannister surrounded the platform. They looked out at the platform in Grand Central Station, at the well-wishers and press who had chosen to stay behind.

Jonathan checked his pocketwatch, smiled at her and slipped his arm around her waist.

The train whistle blew long and loud.

With a jolt, the new Twentieth Century Limited came to life. The fourteen-hour, overnight journey from Chicago to New York had begun.

Jonathan and Darcy braced themselves on the black metal bannister, fully experiencing the moment when the train left the station and rumbled through the dusky Chicago trainyard, picking up speed.

"It's wonderful, Jonathan." She rocked back and forth against him. "I'm glad to be here."

"You are wonderful, lady. Welcome to my dream."

He took her in his arms and kissed her, holding her still against the rhythm of the train. "I love you, Darcy."

"And I love you."

They returned to the parlor car where the throng greeted them with a toast. "To the Twentieth Century."

"A new era."

"Indeed it is," Darcy said quietly.

"A time for us," he said.

Long, happy hours passed in a blur while Darcy and Jonathan enjoyed the company and the ride. There were civilized conversations and a fine meal—with chicken as an alternate choice on the menu—in the dining car. Eventually, the passengers drifted toward the Pullman cars, ready for an evening's repose.

Before she and Jonathan left the parlor for the night, Darcy shared a quiet moment with Mrs. Archibald.

"This is a lovely way to travel," she said. "My late husband and I took a train ride on our honeymoon. To Niagara Falls."

"I'm glad you like it," Darcy said.

"You have given me so very much, Darcy. I can't thank you enough for saving my Renoir. Losing it would have been losing a dream."

Darcy clasped the older woman's crippled hand in hers. "Lately, I seem to be spending much of my time in the dream-saving business."

"It suits you nicely. As does Mr. Hillcroft. You make a very handsome couple."

"Thank you."

She returned to Jonathan's side, reveling in the warm smile he bestowed upon her. "Tired?" he asked.

"Not at all. But I am ready for bed."

They left the late night revelers and jostled their way single file through the narrow hallways in the Pullman section of the train.

Jonathan opened the door to a deluxe suite of two adjoining compartments which had been remodeled in 1902-style. The walls were wainscoted in walnut with flecked brown and blue wallpaper above. The ceiling fixture sported a leaded glass lamp shade. The tables which were affixed to the floor had claw-foot legs and the sofas were plush grey velvet.

Darcy lowered herself onto the sofa. "Beautiful. This compartment is like a tiny corner of the past. A time capsule."

"Glad you like it." He sat beside her. "And I would like to point out that your modern ideas have been thoroughly incorporated. As you suggested, the engine is diesel instead of steam. Fabrics and wallpaper throughout only look old-fashioned. We're talking the most durable scotch-guarded stuff here."

"It's wonderful. I have only one complaint."

"Which is?"

"My feet." She pulled up her long, black skirt to reveal black high-button shoes. "No wonder the women preferred to stay home in those days. These shoes would discourage anybody from traipsing anywhere.''

Jonathan ran a finger around the edge of his high, starched collar. ''I could do without this piece of authenticity.''

While she attacked the laces and yanked off her pointy-toed shoes, he unfastened his necktie and loosened his collar.

Together, they breathed a sigh of relief.

''There is a bit of modern technology in this Pullman,'' he said. ''See if you can find it.''

She studied the walls and floor before her eye came to rest on a control panel on the wall. ''Ah ha!'' She punched a button and immediately jumped. The sofa she'd been sitting upon folded up to make a headboard and a wide double bed descended electronically from the wall.

''Very nice,'' Darcy said, testing the firm mattress. ''I like this. And it suits you.''

''How so?''

''Beneath your proper exterior, there lurks an essentially sexy, modern man.''

''I could say the same thing about you, Darcy.''

''Don't say it, show me.''

He needed no further encouragement. Jonathan enfolded her in his embrace and together they fell onto the bed. His kisses awoke an answering passion in her, as they renewed the sensual promise of their commitment.

The only problem was their old-fashioned clothing.

Jonathan propped himself above her and fumbled at the front of her fancy white blouse. "How many buttons does this thing have?"

"Twenty-five." She folded her hands behind her head. "But wait until you see what I have on underneath."

He groaned. When he had unfastened down to her cleavage, Jonathan leaned forward and placed a warm kiss in the hollow of her throat. He unbuttoned further, revealing a lacey white fabric below. Still lower, the peaks of breasts made taut puckers in the satin.

His fingertips teased her nipples and Darcy felt a tickling in the pit of her stomach. When she unfolded her arms and reached for him, he stopped her. "Lie still," he said. "I'm beginning to enjoy this. It's like unwrapping a Christmas present."

He finished with the blouse, sensually caressing each new satin inch of Darcy that appeared. The long black skirt was easily removed, and Darcy lay before him in a white teddy, garter belt and black stockings.

"This is definitely a fantasy," he murmured.

He peeled off his suit coat and vest. His more conventional shirt was yanked off in an instant.

He leaned over her and unhooked the garters, one by one. Slowly, he rolled her stockings down the length of her legs.

The tension in Darcy built to an unbearable level

as she lay back on the bed, watching him and feeling his touch. The rhythm of the rails rocked her.

He removed the rest of his clothing and stretched out beside her on the bed. Again, she turned toward him, intending to take him in her arms. "Wait," he said.

His hand slid over the satin fabric covering her breasts and stomach. He reached lower. With a deft touch, he unsnapped the crotch of her teddy.

Darcy couldn't stand it anymore. She embraced him furiously. And they made love.

The train seemed to move in sympathy with them. A gentle swaying motion became a fierce forward thrust, surging into a velvet black night.

When finally their passion had subsided and they lay side by side watching the landscape fly past the window of the sleeping compartment, Jonathan nuzzled her ear and whispered, "Why did you come to me, Darcy?"

"I couldn't stay away."

"What about all the details? The complications?"

"I trust that we can work them out." She turned to him and stroked his cheek. "It's like the train. You had to overcome several obstacles to bring this train onto its present course, to fulfill your dream. I have a dream, too. A very romantic dream of loving and being loved. It took me a while to realize it, Jonathan, but you are my dream. My dream come true."

They spent the night discovering the depth of Darcy's dream, nestled in each other's arms on a deluxe car of the new Twentieth Century Limited.

Their time had come. The right time and the right place. Thoroughly modern Darcy had found the moment when she could trust in her fantasies, and Jonathan the dreamer learned that her reality was the sweetest fulfillment of all. Together, heralded by the long, low whistle of the Twentieth Century Limited, they journeyed to a special mythical place where their hearts would be joined forever.

When the train pulled into the station in New York City, it was precisely on schedule.